D1548473

THE

HELLFIRE

BRATS

E. M. Allen

ISBN: 978-1-66786-297-2 (paperback)

ISBN: 978-1-66786-298-9 (eBook)

Dedicated to Cindy for supporting my creative drive my entire life

PROLOGUE

The slight chill in the air signaled the end of the summer of 2018. Steady, practiced hands stayed true to their craft. The old tailor found solace in his work. It had been a long time since he set out on a night like this to hunt his prey. Now he spent his nights on one of his finer passions. Threads of dark cashmere were woven together. Disparate strings were shaped into a fine suit. It was honest work that made more than a pretty penny.

The tailor's name was Charles Pickens. He was well known amongst the east coast elites. Once upon a time he had been a mage of some renown, fighting for the defense of the helpless as a knight of The Celestial Order. Now he spent his days weaving fibers into fancy suits for the wealthy. But what they didn't know was that cotton and cashmere were not the only strings he pulled. In truth, Charles Pickens was also the servant of a certain man.

That man was called Sir Nightwatch. For seventeen years the two had secretly worked together. Between the unbridled talent of Sir Nightwatch, and Pickens own meager set of expertise, the two ran a tight knit group of agents that they bemusingly referred to as Nightwatch. Sir Nightwatch had been the de facto leader. He was younger and stronger than Charles and the entire operation had been his idea. Charles had known Sir Nightwatch for much of the man's life. So he was uniquely attuned to his master's state of being.

Sir Nightwatch was always a cold, analytical fellow watching the world from his perch. He had always been a man of intense focus and superhuman drive. Even so, Charles had sensed a change in him five years ago. Time was, Sir Nightwatch could relax. Time was, Sir Nightwatch would smile. The time that was, ended five years ago, and he always kept whatever happened close to the chest. It was as if he was on a mission. That's the look that had plagued his face these last five years. He started something five years ago. Whatever it was, it seemed to end that very night. For the first time in five years he smiled. It wasn't the soft smile he would give to his subordinates. It was the satisfactory, almost sadistic smile he had after every successful hunt.

He was dressing himself in his usual mission garb. A long black coat drifted to his legs, his face wrapped in a silver scarf. The clothes he sported were black as night and thick as fog. He quickly slid on a pair of dark rider gloves and finished off the set with a pointed hat over his dark hair.

"Going somewhere?" Charles was usually the first one he told of any new developments. In his age, Charles had taken it upon himself to be the organization's record keeper. He detested the idea of his master keeping him out of the loop. It made it far more difficult to manage the particulars of everyone's assignments if he didn't know as much detail as the devil himself.

"The time has come to collect on a debt." Sir Nightwatch's words were cryptic. "I am going to St. Louis."

"St. Louis?" Charles blinked. St. Louis, for as wrought with crime as it tended to be, was one city that had never needed Sir Nightwatch himself to visit. At least not since one of his most trusted agents had taken to the town. "Whatever for? I'm sure Master Rogers has everything quite under control."

"It's not a threat. It's quite the opposite." Sir Nightwatch said as he stepped onto the balcony. "Five years…five years ago I made a promise and it's time to fulfill that obligation." His fiery amber eyes bored directly into the soul of his comrade. Charles still didn't have the slightest idea of what he was talking about. A debt? A promise? Something in St. Louis?

Sure, he knew the significance of that city, more than the usual mage at the very least. It was small, but historically, it was called the Gateway City for numerous reasons. It was also very important to Sir Nightwatch. Charles had gleaned that much over the years. Of the half-dozen mages under their employ, Rodgers was the youngest and the one Sir Nightwatch had the most contact with. There were also a few theories Charles had formulated after some research into that area. But the tailor had not been able to confirm his hypotheses. Sir Nightwatch had managed to keep a great number of secrets even from his closest confidant.

"Well then…" Charles picked his next words carefully. "Send Master Rogers my regards."

"If I see him, I will." Sir Nightwatch said with a tip of his hat. "Prepare to open up a new file. I'll fill you in with the details when the deed is done." With that he left, jumping off the balcony and taking to the sky like an owl. He flew westward, away from the city, and to the place that held so much importance for him.

Yes, Charles recalled the last time he visited St. Louis was five years ago as well. Perhaps it had something to do with the prolonged shift in his mood. Whatever it was, Master Rogers didn't seem to know either, and he was the only Nightwatch agent in the area. Perhaps this night would be more enlightening than he initially thought. Time would tell. Sir Nightwatch kept his secrets, but he always told his tailor eventually.

CHAPTER 1

Welcome to Shadowbrooke

As one volume ends, so too must one begin. That's what was on Oliver Turner's mind the further he got from Springfield. It wasn't the first time he had moved from one town to another. In fact, he was returning to the town where he was born. But this move felt different. Perhaps it was the end of the summer coinciding with this move. Perhaps it was because he would be beginning his freshman year in a town where he was a stranger. Perhaps it was a feeling of nostalgia for the place his parents had met. In truth all three of these sensations coalesced into a feeling of unease for the boy.

It had been his father's idea. Oliver had very few memories of his early life. His family had moved away from that area before he had started kindergarten. Even so, his mother still worked in Shadowbrook until she died in 2012. When that happened, he and his father moved to a smaller house in Springfield. For the last five years, his father talked about moving back up when the time was right. That time had come at the dawn of Oliver's first year in high school. Oliver had protested of course. He had a difficult time making friends and if that wasn't bad enough he was prone to illness. He had only just started to live comfortably in Springfield and was looking forward to attending high school with the few friends he had managed to make.

Everything was murky. The road ahead was covered in a layer of drab gray. Weather in the midwest is always fickel and ridiculous. It was the end of summer yet it felt like fall. Billy Turner was feeling the mood. The trip had started off sunny and cheery. He had been excited to make this pilgrimage back to the city. Yet he had slowly become more solemn as he drove the moving van closer to Shadowbrooke.

Billy Turner had a soft face covered in hair. His blue eyes had become increasingly hollow over forty years of his life. He quietly mouthed the words to the song on the radio as they approached their destination. It had only been a few turns off the highway before reaching their new home on Hamilton.

The house was a quaint suburban structure. The paint was fresh like an older woman's makeup before a night on the town. The sidewalk leading up to the porch showed its age. The owners had done well to keep the cracks from engulfing the home but time was one thing no carpenter could combat against forever.

"Well, we're here." Billy said.

No noise could be heard from the Turners as they moved their boxes inside. They let the music of the radio be the only sound. If the outside of the house was an admirable effort to stave off the assault of time, the inside was a logbook of the prior residents. The walls were freshly painted and the relatively spacious floors were clean. But there were also stains on the carpet, old scars on the counters, chips in the ceiling tile and other such records of accidental anecdotes.

The living room was the largest room. There was a hallway on the opposite side of the room from the door. The hallway had four doors along it. The first was a bathroom. Then there were the two bedrooms. The last door was an office that could be used for any number of things. A wall separated the hallway from the dining room. Both paths met up in the kitchen. The kitchen housed a back door leading to a porch and a sizable backyard.

There was also a basement door in the kitchen. The basement itself was musty but had more than enough room for storage, laundry and a game room if Oliver was lucky.

It took us a few hours to move everything in. Oliver picked out the room closest to the bathroom and got it situated. He placed his bed in one corner. His desk with his computer, TV and games was hooked up along the wall near the door.

"I'm going to go ahead and make pizza." His father said.

"Alright." Oliver said as he turned on his computer. The rest of his belongings could wait another day. Night had already begun to fall and he was tired of the long day of labor.

"You need to go to bed early tonight." His father reminded him.

"I know."

"I'm being serious. We gotta register you for classes tomorrow."

"I know!" The teen's voice was more petulant.

The next day started frantically. Oliver was never a morning person. He detested coffee and didn't like the kind of tea his father did. He also had a hard time thinking of something to wear. He settled on a plain white t-shirt and jeans. He didn't really want to draw too much attention to himself. Being the new guy was going to be hard enough.

The school was a lot bigger than his last school. One of the secretaries handed him a map of the building, a schedule, and a list of classes he had to pick from. Oliver had to walk around the school and get his schedule figured out.

"We should probably knock the easy ones out first." Billy said. "You have to fill out six hours of classes. One for each core subject, one elective and then band."

"There's only one period for band class." Oliver said as he scanned the page. He quickly found the room number, its location and then led the way.

When they arrived in the band room there was one other family there. The father of this other family was ten-years Billy's senior. His only noteworthy feature was the tuft of curly blonde hair atop his head. His two daughters were seventeen and fifteen respectively. The elder daughter was preparing for her third year at the school.

At a glance you wouldn't be able to tell they were siblings. They had nothing in common. It was as if their father's traits had been split evenly among the girls with no overlap in their appearance. The elder daughter was blonde with her father's curly hair. She was roughly five-foot-eight-inches, making her two inches taller than Oliver and only two inches shorter than Billy. The younger girl was short, athletic with dark hair and brown eyes. Her head was round like her father's which stood in stark contrast to the thinner jawline of her older sister. She was also the shortest person in the room, measuring at five-foot-two-inches.

It was the younger girl who first noticed the Turners' entrance. A hint of recognition crossed her features as she nudged her father. The two older men locked eyes and both men saw their blue eyes light up.

"Tyler?" Billy was the one to break the silence.

"Is that you Billy?" Tyler said. "Long time no see!"

"Who's this guy?" The blonde daughter asked.

"Oh, an old work friend from years ago. A friend of a friend really." Tyler was unsure how exactly to best summarize his history with Billy Turner without dredging up some painful memories.

"Neat." The younger daughter was satisfied enough with that explanation. She locked eyes with Oliver, sizing up her would-be classmate. Even though she was a smidge shorter than the boy, it was he who relented. He had never had much skill in talking to girls and if he were as vocal as he was honest he would have to admit that he found both girls to be quite good looking.

"I heard through the grapevine you were moving up here." Tyler said.

"Yeah, it was time for us to get back to our roots." Billy said. "Oh this is my son Oliver. I don't think you ever had the chance to meet him." He pushed me forward. "If you did it was too long for him to remember."

"Nope never had the pleasure." Tyler said. "You remember Brittany?" He gestured to the older girl. Oliver's face began to redden as he was forced to take in more of her features. The word bombshell crossed his mind as his eyes gravitated up her body. The tight jeans and yellow tanktop didn't do much to hide her features.

"And I'm Rachel Rune." The shorter girl jumped between the curious boy and her older sister. She too was wearing jeans but the top she sported was much more modest.

"O-Oliver." The boy stammered his introduction and shook her hand.

"So you're new. I'm a freshman here starting this year but I have my sister to show me the ropes." She tapped my arm.

"I'm a freshman too." I said as I averted her gaze. Her wide brown eyes looked like they were trying to see through me as quickly as they could.

"Man, I can't believe Brittany is all grown up." Billy said. "And I didn't even know you had a second kid. Does that mean..."

The band teacher stepped out of his office with a handful of forms thus interrupting the reunion. Tyler breathed a sigh of relief. Now that the Turners had returned there would be plenty of time to catch up. The past sixteen years had been filled with many blessings and curses for Tyler Rembrandt and his family. This was neither the time nor the place for such stories.

"You must be Mr. Turner." He said. Mr. Berry the band teacher was an older African-American man who bore a striking resemblance to a walrus.

"Yeah." Billy said.

"I take it your son plays an instrument." Mr. Berry said.

"Yes, he played percussion in middle school." Billy answered before Oliver could speak up.

"Can he do xylophone and other things like that?"

"Yes...I can." Oliver answered for himself that time.

"Great! My star keyboard percussionist graduated last year."

"Yeah, I play percussion too!" Rachel said. Oliver was not expecting the abrupt invasion of his personal space and so her sudden closeness caused his heart to skip a beat. "But I've never really done xylophone."

"Well, I'll be glad to have both of you here." Mr. Berry said. He wrote both names down on one of his forms. After that he talked to the two fathers about some of the activities they would be doing. Meanwhile Rachel continued to inquire about Oliver and his schedule. She looked to compare the two only to find that he was only getting started.

After that the Turners left. As they did Billy mumbled to himself about the names of those girls. It was a curious thing that one of them had a different last name. Oliver figured there was a reason behind it but wasn't one to push for such knowledge. Billy Turner knew better because the last name of the younger girl rang familiar.

Oliver filled out the rest of his schedule and met with the various teachers he would be working with. It looked daunting, if for no other reason than how much ground he would have to cover in the short time between classes. But it was something he would have to get used to. On the social front, he still had his reservations but Rachel seemed nice at the very least. She also seemed like the type to put in the effort to make friends herself. Oliver wasn't sure how to feel about that. He had only known her nary a minute and she had already gotten closer than he was realistically comfortable with.

He wasn't even sure if he wanted to make any friends here. He just wanted to get through high school and leave. Aside from Rachel, nothing about that school seemed particularly inviting. Even then Oliver couldn't help but wonder if his classmate had ulterior motives or if she truly acted that way around everyone. The majority of the teachers had been cold and disinterested toward him. Oliver was fretting over every detail. His lack of confidence fed into his own self-destructive neurosis, which made his penchant for illness worsen. He had to focus on what positives he could in order to stave away depression. This feeling persisted until the first day of school.

CHAPTER 2

Bartleby of the Storm

It was the first day of school and Oliver could feel the change in his gut. Missouri was no stranger to freak weather. Most people in the midwest wouldn't pay any mind to a looming storm cloud unless it somehow impeded their plans.

Billy was watching the news. The man on the screen was none other than Damien Crow. He was the host of Blackfire News broadcasting from Chicago. Everyone in America had at least heard of him. Usually he was on in the evening, commenting on politics and the actions of The Celestial Order. For whatever reason he had decided to pop in as a special guest on someone else's program. Oliver may not have paid it any mind but if he had, he would have been privy to an omen of things to come.

Damien Crow was talking about a growing refugee crisis across The Rift. He had been putting in extra time to advocate justice for those persecuted by The Celestial Order. Oliver, like any boy his age, had an interest in the mystical aspects of the world but he had never once met a member of The Celestial Order. So to him, hearing about magic and monsters was no different than hearing about European politics. It had always seemed so distant in his mind.

Upon arriving at school, the teenager swallowed his resolve and pushed on towards his homeroom. Not five seconds upon entering the room he was greeted by a familiar face once again getting too close for comfort.

"Hello!" Rachel was flanked by two other athletic kids. One of them was a tall boy twice Oliver's size. The other was a stout woman who wasn't much smaller. Rachel was quite short but next to these two she looked positively miniscule. "It looks like we're in the same homeroom."

"Rachel, right?" He responded.

"Ahem." She smiled. "My name is Rachel Rune. So long as you don't shoot off at the mouth like an idiot we'll do just fine."

"I'm Joey." The boy said. "I like working on cars."

"Aayla, and I'm secretly a nerd." The trio ended their introduction.

"Not much of a secret if that's how you introduce yourself." Oliver said to himself. The boy then cleared his throat and gave his own introduction. "I'm Oliver. And I…guess I'm new around here."

"Well new kid we're all freshmen so we're all kinda new kids if you think about it." Rachel may have been the smallest one of the bunch but she commanded the attention of those around her. This boisterous personality was honed from years of trying to compete with her older sister and pull any potential friends towards her. She was the kind of person people gravitated towards. Even Oliver, for all his resistance, couldn't help but smile watching her. "The three of us are all part of the same group. We all grew up on the same street and went to all the same schools."

"That's cool." Oliver said. He admired how they approached him. It would be easy to make friends with people who were so personable. But he couldn't help but have his doubts. What place was there for him if they had been friends for so long?

"Tell us about yourself." Joey said. The dopey-eyed teen may have been the simplest of the bunch. His mellow voice did not seem to match his impressive physique and the combination was disarming for Oliver.

"I like playing video games and I guess I like sports." In truth Oliver liked watching sports. He hadn't played any since he was in elementary.

He only brought it up because the trio were clearly athletes and would be happy to share that interest.

"If you want we can always use more people on the track team." Rachel said. "Since you're new it'll probably help you make some friends. Tryouts are later in the month but I'm already part of the team."

"Wait, how does that work?" He asked.

Rachel nodded with pride in unison with her subordinates.

"Rachel's kind of a superstar track athlete." Joey said.

"I may have beaten a bunch of records in middle school." Rachel said. "Anyway, the bell is about to ring. So that's the end of my shilling. You look like you'd do well there." She punctuated the conversation with a wink.

The rest of the day went off without a hitch. Sharing the same home-room, lunch and a few classes with Rachel helped ease the tension in Oliver's mind. There was nothing else worth remembering from that day. But all this stood in contrast to the turn Oliver's life would take that night.

Sleep had never come easy for Oliver. As stated before, he was chronically ill as a child and though his sickness had eased up over the years, it always seemed to cling to him during the dark hours of the night. During the worst nights, his mother would stay up with him until his body finally felt sleep's embrace. But that was no longer possible. It had been five years since her passing and Oliver had to find ways to take care of himself.

12:00 am. Midnight the numbers taunted. But it was no illness or restlessness that stirred him awake this time. It was the sound of thunder. It was a strange storm. Lightning lit across the sky, streaking from cloud to cloud. Not a single drop of rain fell though. Freak storms were common-place in the midwest so few people would have paid it much mind.

But this one had arrived out of nowhere. Nothing of this magnitude had been part of the forecast. The clouds that had drifted in the early hours of the day were now swirling in a violent maelstrom. The darkest clouds hung directly above that little house on Hamilton street.

Oliver climbed out of bed to watch the storm. Perhaps he would find some solace in the chaos that reigned outside. What he found was far more than mere solace. He stepped out onto the back porch and saw the swirl of shadow, the dancing light, and the very world around him begin to warp.

ZZZAP! The lightning bolt struck mere feet away from Oliver. The shock of thunder knocked him back through the open door. He heard his father call for him. Before the teen responded he was captivated by a glint of silver attached to a shadowy form. And beneath it, stood the most horrible thing Oliver had ever seen.

The mere sight of it chilled Oliver to the bone. It froze him so thoroughly he could see his breath. The monster's insectoid wings had been charred black. Six spindly legs twitched trying to regain its balance. It wrestled with the pit of darkness that obscured most of its features. Oliver only got small glimpses. His eyes refused to blink as he tried to make sense of what he was watching.

As soon as he saw that the monstrosity had a human-like face he knew what was happening. For the first time in his life he was seeing a battle between mages. One was a demoran that had taken the form of an insectoid arbiter of destruction. The other was a twisting mass of shadow with fiery orange eyes.

BZZT POW! Lightning erupted from the ground and pierced the sky with light. The shadow twisted, shrunk and vanished as the creature stood back up. The top part was vaguely humanoid. In the fading light its skin looked as blue as the lightning bolt. One arm ended in a giant pincer and the other was lined with keratin spikes.

A more well-informed viewer would recognize this creature as Bartleby of the Storm. He had been high on America's most wanted list. He was a reprehensible demon mage who had been engaged in human trafficking and illegal experiments. Truly he had been an insect demoran who mutilated himself in pursuit of greater power. And now he was here, in Shadowbrooke.

Freed from the shadow that had bound it, the demon laughed and spoke in a tongue that was beyond Oliver's comprehension. "Zieg Furcal Nephilima Nihahaha." Its grotesque pincer opened and a sphere of blue mana began to build up. The creature had taken direct aim at the teenager. There was no craven anger or thirst for destruction in his eyes. The monster was taking personal satisfaction in the thought of snuffing the life of this boy.

"Oliver get down!" Billy managed to reach his son and pull him to the floor just in time. A wave of electricity blasted through the house and tore through it like glass. Everything in the attack's path shattered like glass, not just the sliding door. The table, the cabinet, all of it had cracked and scattered into a pile of sharp debris.

"Krush kia Daphne nihaha." Bartleby once again spoke. While Oliver still had no understanding of the language one word did stick out. The creature had said the name of his mother.

"Ollie." Billy clung tightly to his boy as he tried lifting the both of them up. Another radiant blast fired from the creature's claw only to be stopped by the mysterious shadowy void that had been present earlier.

This time, the figure took a more human form. The mass of shadows was in fact a coat. The streak of silver was his scarf. A pointed hat topped his head. The man in black had saved the Turners from certain death. No stray bolt of electricity got past him. His cloak of shadow spread to catch anything that would cause the people harm. Eventually the attack faded and this savior of the night fell to his knees in exhaustion.

"Nihahaha." Bartleby laughed as he walked forward and spoke again. This time the voice was groggy but his words were clear. To taunt the mage he had switched to speaking English. "Even you have your limits. You're not so scary when you're on your knees."

With a single motion, Bartleby clutched the mage and hoisted him off the ground. This would-be hero struggled against the claw but failed to break free. Instead, he slammed his hand into his opponent's throat and attempted to strangle him. Orange eyes burned in determination to kill the criminal before he could be killed himself. Bartleby had the advantage. His thick carapace made it difficult for the mage to sever his breath. Meanwhile the demon gathered energy into his claw again. This time the blast would rip his opponent in half and finish him off for good.

Oliver's fight or flight syndrome kicked in. He had never considered himself a brave soul. He had been lucky enough never to put his mettle to the test. It was actually a calculated risk that drove him to action. He knew nothing of magic and neither did his father. If they had any hope of seeing the next sunrise, Oliver needed to do everything he could to save the man who had saved him.

His father pleaded for him to stop. A golden glow flashed throughout the street. Oliver's knuckles burst as they impacted the spiked shell of Bartleby. The coolness of blood rained between the torn fingers. The punch had landed on the monster's claw, loosening its grip ever so slightly.

"Foolish boy!" The creature shouted. "Nihahaha, you call that a punch?"

"I call it a distraction." It was the shadowy savior's turn to speak. His body erupted into darkness and slithered out of the monster's grip. The darkness took the shape of numerous skewers and binds that impaled Bartleby and bound him once again.

"Damn you." The monster coughed out. The mage put a reassuring hand on Oliver's shoulders. A glint of gun metal emerged from the shadows of his other hand. His gloved hand took aim and squeezed on the trigger.

Bang! Bang! The two bullets leapt from the barrel but didn't reach their mark. Bartleby broke free from his restraints once again and distanced himself from the mage. The man closed the distance in the blink of an eye. His fist cracked against Bartleby's thorax. Shadows once again wrapped around the creature. This time the man himself rolled over Bartleby's towering body. He sat on the back of the demon's insectoid body. His arms ensnared the monster in a headlock.

"Checkmate." The two bullets from earlier circled back and hit the side of the monster's head. Blood splattered from the wounds as it screamed in pain.

"Bastard!" Was the monster's final words before the shadowy figure pierced it again. This time a wave of electricity tore the creature apart, burning it and scattering what was left into the wind. When there was no trace of the monster left, the world returned to normal. The damage that was done to the house was peeled away. The world around them no longer bent towards the sky. It was quiet as if nothing had happened. But the man in black stayed standing.

"Evening gentlemen." The figure removed his hat revealing nicely combed black hair underneath. "Allow me to properly introduce myself. I am Sir Nightwatch."

"I know who you are." Billy huffed as he marched over to the man. "You said it was over. You said it was safe." He grabbed Sir Nightwatch's arm.

"I said...that everything was ready." Sir Nightwatch corrected as he forcibly removed Billy's hand from his arm. "The world is always dangerous for our kind." Blue eyes questioned orange. There was history there to be sure. But the two had never shared much in conversation and so Billy had no choice but to relent and hear the enigmatic mage out.

"You're a...you're a mage!" Oliver was still in disbelief at what he had seen.

"I am." Sir Nightwatch nodded as he returned his hat to his head.

"He was a friend of your mother's." Billy revealed. The questions started to pile up in Oliver's head but he was patient. He had already surmised that much just from what little he understood of Bartleby.

"A professional acquaintance." Sir Nightwatch said. "People on our level in our line of work have little luxury for friends."

"Wait, Mom was a mage too?"

"Yes." Billy admitted. "But she never wanted you exposed to that world."

"Wise choice given the heritage." Sir Nightwatch added. "Though the boy is fifteen now, surely he is ready to learn."

"Learn what?" Oliver asked.

"Mr. Turner, with your permission of course I would like to recruit the boy into the Nightwatch Organization."

"The what?" He questioned his father. He took a deep breath and sighed.

"Better you than anyone else I suppose." Billy lamented. "There's not very many who would be willing to teach someone like him."

"Given the heritage." Sir Nightwatch nodded again. "Tell me, what is your name, boy?"

"Oliver...Oliver Turner." Oliver answered. "What is Nightwatch?" While many groups of mages had made their way to Oliver's ears. Namely The Celestial Order and Japan's Onikoroshi. Nightwatch was one he was completely unfamiliar with. He had never seen nor heard of them or of anyone matching this man's description.

"The Nightwatch Organization, it's a small yet hardy group dedicated to the defense of the defenseless." Sir Nightwatch stated his case.

"Like superheroes?" Oliver asked.

"If you insist." Sir Nightwatch mused. "We fight monsters, spirits and any mage that wishes to do harm to the people of this world. Like Bartleby there, he was an enemy of your mother that had been waiting for your return for quite some time so that he may take revenge. He was a demon, but one that had given up any moral fiber in favor of becoming a true monster."

"Oliver." Billy cut in. "If you join this organization, there's no going back. It'll be dangerous." He put his hands on his son's arms and looked him in the eye. There was nothing but curiosity on his youthful face this time.

"I am no fool Mr. Turner." Sir Nightwatch cut back in. "I will not be able to directly oversee his training. One of my best agents lives in the area and he is only a little older than Oliver. He will oversee the boy's training." Sir Nightwatch began to walk away. "He will approach you tomorrow so be ready. And Mr. Turner, because he still lives under your roof and by extension your rules, you will decide in what capacity he works with us. But I implore you, leave the details of his training to my agent and I."

"Yes Sir." Billy nodded.

"Until we meet again." Sir Nightwatch looked to the sky. The form of his coat began to twist and mold once again.

"Wait!" Oliver shouted. "You're leaving already?"

"I'm a very busy man, Oliver Turner. I'll be in touch but I must take my leave. Welcome to the Organization. Your mother would be proud. I look forward to seeing you live up to that great potential you inherited from her."

"I...won't disappoint." The young boy said. As Sir Nightwatch gave one last nod, Oliver could see the traces of a warm smile emerging from the silver scarf. Sir Nightwatch had a keen eye for talent and he knew Oliver's circumstances. Most people who wished to do magic would start learning at a far earlier age. But there was a reason Oliver couldn't and that same reason was why Sir Nightwatch was confident he would catch up to his peers in a short time. But that too held its risks.

CHAPTER 3

Donald "Dodger" Rogers

On the edges of Shadowbrooke laid a house no different from any other in the area. Its main distinguishing feature was the expensive car that was parked in the driveway throughout the night. For any passerby there was nothing exceptional about this house. And if someone were to take a peek inside they would see a very typical bachelor pad. There was nothing about the house or its layout that could be seen as extraordinary. What was extraordinary was how the inside of the house never changed.

This was because there was only a single resident and he hardly spent enough time at home to make it a mess. Peculiar still, this single resident was seventeen-year-old Donald Rogers. The boy who preferred to be called Dodger did not live with his parents. His bills were paid for by a benefactor. He had never attended any parent-teacher conferences. Nobody else had been seen in the house in over three years.

Many of his classmates, particularly the ladies, had questioned him on this topic. The teen never talked about his home life or anything he did after school, much to the dismay of the girls who fawned over him. There were only a handful that even knew that he had been orphaned at an early age, raised in New York by a tailor, and now lived on his own. His living expenses were paid in full by the one he truly served. All his bills and expenses were taken care of by an enigmatic figure named Simon Saize–one of many aliases denoting that most elusive mage, Sir Nightwatch.

Dodger had been taken in by Sir Nightwatch when he was too young to remember. When the master mage was confident in Dodger's ability to fend for himself, he set him up here near St. Louis to be an extension of Nightwatch's will. As part of that will, Dodger had a certain meeting to attend. The boy who was a student of Nightwatch was to be an instructor for the newest member of the gang.

As he prepared for the day he used telekinesis whenever he could. Using one's will to move objects was simple for a mage. It was often one of the first skills a prospective mage learned. Dodger was always quite good at it and treated this morning routine as an excuse to keep his skill sharp.

He wore the clothes typical of a youth in this day and age. There was just one last piece that he rarely parted ways with. He was an avid baseball offianado and he never left the house without showing support for the St. Louis Cardinals.

The teen wasn't used to rolling into school early. He was an exceptional academic but a horrible student. He rarely paid attention in class and would often skip out on classes that didn't interest him. With the education he received while living in New York, he probably didn't even need to attend classes. But schools were useful to him. It was the best place to meet people his own age. These people liked to gossip, oftentimes had their own skill sets and expertise all of which had proven useful to the monster hunter. It also gave him a semblance of the normal life he had been robbed of before.

Very few of the teachers cared for him. The school had a no-hats policy that he broke as easily as he breathed. None of the staff appreciated his antics as a person. Most of the teachers merely tolerated his tardiness and disregard for school rules simply because he always had some of the best test scores. This stood in contrast to his homework, which was always perfect when done but wasn't done at all half the time.

His first order of business was to scout out the cafeteria. The cafeteria had three main sections. The lower section held the majority of the tables as well as the food line. Then there was a section off to the side with a few more tables. Finally, there was the raised section with an extended counter lined with stools bolted to the ground. It was here he made his start.

It was also here that he had his first social interaction of the day. One girl had taken note of his early arrival and knew him well enough to know this was not the norm. There was still twenty minutes until class started and yet Dodger was here, thirty minutes earlier than his usual arrival. This girl was none other than Brittany Rembrandt, Dodger's classmate and the closest thing he had to a real friend. Brittany had taken a liking to Dodger as soon as they first met and had been trying to insert herself more into his life ever since.

"What brings you here so early Dodger?" Brittany asked as she snatched the hat off his head. Dodger gave her a once over. It was a sight for sore eyes to be sure, but one that was just as much a distraction as it was a pleasure.

"Don't worry about it." He stole the cap back from her and continued his hunt for this new agent. Even though she knew about his after school activities, and had even gone out with him on many occasions, she did not know about Nightwatch and therefore had no reason to be involved in this particular affair.

"Oh I know." She leaned in and poked his arm. "You're looking for Eliza aren't you?"

It made sense that Brittany would think that. Most of the time when Dodger was on the prowl it was to whatever destination the resident Arch Knight of The Celestial Order was headed.

"Ha, she wishes." Dodger responded with an eye roll. He did not care for Eliza in the slightest and tried his best never to actively seek her out. But he was a mage and a freelance monster hunter as far as anyone was concerned. And so it was only natural that he would cross paths with her on a regular basis.

Eliza was in fact in the cafeteria. Dodger had sensed her cold mess of a disposition the moment he stepped on school grounds. She had also taken note of his presence at the same time and did her best to ignore him. But when her name escaped the lips of her classmate, she decided to pay him a visit.

"No hats inside school Dodger." She sneered as she passed the pair. Dodger was tempted to take the rubber ball out of his pocket and throw it at the back of her head, just to annoy her. But he chose not to make a scene. "That's what I thought." She said as he put the ball back in his pocket. Eliza might not have been able to glimpse the future as he did, but she was still quite possibly the strongest mage in Missouri, as low of a bar as that may be.

"You two fighting again?" Brittany asked.

"I'd be truly worried if we weren't." Dodger joked. That was the worrisome truth about his rocky connection to Eliza. Because they walked similar roads for different gangs, they were bound to compete. After that encounter Dodger had still failed to see anyone matching the description he was given so he decided to lean on one of Brittany's skills. "Anyway, heard there was a new kid around, about the same age as your sister."

"Oh, you must mean Oliver." Brittany said. "My sister already did her thing and pulled him into her group. What do you want with him?"

"Well, if he's going to be hanging around you girls it's best I get acquainted."

"What's your game, Dodger?"

"Baseball, but you already knew that."

"Looking for new players? Why don't you join the school team?"

"I'd rather play on my own time and call the shots." Dodger said.

"You're hiding something." That was putting it lightly. She knew about the activities and methodology Dodger partook in but not the reasoning. She liked it better thinking he was just a concerned citizen playing hero rather than knowing he did the legwork for an enigmatic and secretive figure.

"Well, it's not like we're dating. I don't have any reason to tell you all my secrets." That was a typical response from him. Neither of them were the dating type. He believed it could be detrimental to his health to let someone get that close and she hated being tied down.

Just as he had said that, he spotted a kid matching the description. Blonde hair, blue eyes, short for a boy and just as Brittany had said he was accompanied by Joey—one of the guys Dodger always saw orbiting Rachel Rune. Dodger did one last thing to confirm that this was him. As a mage he had access to three branches of power. These branches together were called the tria-ethos and it's what gave mages their superhuman abilities. Dodger specialized in the ethos referred to as his sensus. This gave him a wider field of view, enhanced senses and the ability to perceive the mana that served as the energy source of mages. And this kid had a ton of mana inside him, enough to even make Eliza jealous. But it was also fragmented, raw, unrefined and locked deep within the boy.

Brittany had dabbled in the mystic arts and was attuned enough to see what Dodger was doing. She worried for the boy. She knew too well the risks that came with hunting monsters and battling mages. It was a risk she was willing to take. She considered herself strong and after years of martial arts training and boxing she had the record to prove it. She had volunteered and Dodger turned her away, yet this kid who looked like he had never been in a real fight piqued his interest. Brittany didn't have the faintest clue why nor did she pay that much mind. She trusted Dodger but took grievance with the thought of forcing a kid into that life.

"Dodger, if you're looking to corrupt that kid..."

"Corrupt is a fun word, let's go with that." He jumped over the railing into the lowest part of the cafeteria. Seconds later he was finally face to face with his target. Upon seeing the older teen, Oliver realized the difference eight inches made.

"Hello?" Dodger made the first greeting. It took Oliver a second to realize what was going on. Before he could even ask, Dodger silenced him and took control of the situation. Their business was on a need to know basis and Joey was not someone who needed to know. "I never got to properly introduce myself last night. Donald Roger, you can just call me Dodger. And no hard feelings about last night. For what it's worth, I think this is a golden opportunity to build a healthy friendship. You said you were new in town."

"I'm Oliver Turner. It's a pleasure to meet you. Er, I mean properly this time." Dodger was going to have to work with him on his honest streak. Agents of Nightwatch had to know how and when to keep their mouths shut.

"What happened last night?" Joey asked. The dopey athlete was having a hard time thinking of a reason why the older kid would have approached Oliver so quickly.

"Don't worry about it for now." Dodger had no interest in Joey or anyone else Rachel surrounded herself with. "Oliver, meet me at the flagpole after school and we'll talk about it while I show you around."

Dodger took his leave. As he did he could hear Joey inquiring further but the boy had wisened up. He made some excuse about getting lost and running into Dodger. Spontaneous storytelling was something far more in Oliver's wheel house. Dodger was half tempted to stay close and listen but his attention was pulled away by another presence. He didn't even have to turn the corner to know who was right around the corner with her back against the wall.

"Bold introduction, even for you." The voice belonged to the other member of The Celestial Order that was stationed here. Basal Knight Amelia Petrochilos, despite being one day older than Dodger and six months older than Eliza, was the arch knight's subordinate. "You know, usually in a place like this, the new kid wouldn't attract such attention early on."

Eliza's leal hound was one person Dodger worried about more than the arch knight. Eliza was a magnitude stronger than her and Amelia made no secret that she was content serving her. But Amelia had the build and physique befitting of her amazonian heritage. She didn't need to be as talented of a mage as Eliza to do her job.

"Well, Amelia, if you must know his parents and I go way back." The half-truth successfully appeased her. Make no mistake, Nightwatch had its eyes on Oliver Turner right out the gate entirely based on how powerful his mother was. Mana had a tendency to run bright in blood. Children of powerful mages were almost always powerful mages in their own right. And Oliver's mother had been an associate of Sir Nightwatch.

"I find that hard to believe." Amelia stated as she left her perch against the wall. "Just be careful. If you are trying to recruit him for whatever it is you think you're accomplishing, we might have to intervene."

"Why don't you stay out of my business." Dodger dropped the pretense. Things like subtlety and subterfuge weren't in the knight's skillset. She had no knowledge of Nightwatch but she knew about Dodger. She had anticipated his words thus far. She expected him to make up lies and excuses the sort of which she wouldn't be able to linger on without a thorough investigation. So she was taken by surprise when he rounded the corner to confront her.

"You always poke your nose in our business." She looked him in the eye for the first time in the conversation. Dodger was taller than most guys and Amelia was only a few inches shorter than him. Her olive skin was ripened from years of physical training. Emerald eyes complimented her bright scarlet hair though that coloration was an aesthetic choice on the knight's part and not her natural appearance. A man of less resolve may have even been intimidated by her piercing emerald gaze but Dodger wasn't like most. He was the only one in the whole school who could rival Amelia or Eliza.

"Never got any complaints before, at least not directly from you." He noted as he leaned forward, challenging her gaze. That was where she differed from her superior. She was far more willing to tolerate him and welcome his aid than Eliza was. Had this been Eliza, Dodger would have already relented. Amelia may have secretly scared him more than anyone at the school, but she was also more amicable. She was easier to approach and have an honest conversation with. But that attitude tended to be a double-edged sword. Dodger dreaded the day when the knight would actually snap at him.

"Well, it's my duty to protect the people." Amelia caved as she often did when challenged in conversation. "I'd feel terrible if you let something bad happen to him."

"I'm sure you would, and your boss would hate to be saddled with the blame."

"She's not that cold." She said halfheartedly.

"I'll see you around Red." Dodger said. A few seconds later the bell rang and it was off to class. The day had just started and Dodger had already fallen back under the suspicion of The Celestial Order. He and Oliver had a long way to go and if the knights were going to interfere then that would complicate things.

CHAPTER 4

Of Baseball and Basics

One of the great mysteries of Shadowbrooke Highschool was whether Dodger was a lazy genius or a mere conman. Shadowbrooke was the gathering place of nearly two-thousand students and yet a few people had inevitably found their way to infamy. This was bound to happen when you also had two members of The Celestial Order receiving their formal education there. Knights of The Celestial Order were only ever in population centers along The Rift that separated the human world from the one controlled by demons and inhabited by monsters. And so while very few were famous across the globe, they were all heralded as heroes in whatever town they resided.

That fame was extended to anyone who got close. It had been an error in judgment that led to Dodger being so noteworthy. It was during his seventh-grade year that he first met Eliza and Amelia. The next day at school he had challenged Eliza to a duel only to be thrown to the floor and threatened by Amelia. Nobody had forgotten that day and Dodger had lived the past four years in infamy as the punk who thought he could fight a mage. And now Oliver was on the cusp of making a similar mistake.

Oliver and Dodger knew little about each other. Oliver had gotten some of the basics from Joey and Rachel. Dodger had been made aware of Oliver's background when Sir Nightwatch first tasked him with this job. Dodger had never taught before but he was taught by some of the best and so he did what they did and started with a question about his own forte.

"So, what do you think of baseball?"

"Baseball? I don't see how that's important." Oliver was very familiar with the sport and had even played a little bit of it when he was in elementary. That made Dodger's job easier. After hearing Oliver's background there was one more pertinent question Dodger needed answering.

"Cardinals fan?"

"Yeah."

"Good man."

"Thought you'd be a Dodgers fan." The joke was easy to make given his name and one he had heard too many times to count.

"Smartass." He smirked. "Baseball is what we call a good frame of reference for what's going to happen."

"My training?"

"Precisely. You won't be able to throw a fireball– at least not without burning your hand off–until you get a grasp on the fundamentals. Just like how you won't be able to hit a homerun until you know how to properly hold the bat."

Dodger had driven Oliver to a baseball field to begin his training. The field itself looked like it had seen better days. Patches of dirt dotted the matts of grass. There was a crescent shaped fence that hung over home plate, separating it from the rotted wooden stands. A poet would probably use this as an illustration for how old and deteriorated the town was. Or at least use it to highlight how thin the city's budget was.

Dodger directed Oliver to home plate and removed a large bag from the trunk of his car. There was nothing extraordinary about the bag. It contained basic equipment such as gloves, bats, balls as well as a set of catcher's gear. The last thing he removed from the back was a large plastic bucket filled with various balls. Most of them were baseballs but there were also a number of softballs and tennis balls.

"Magic, sorcery, witchcraft…" He started as he set the bucket and bats down on the ground. He snapped his fingers multiple times and with each snap a ball flung into the air and hovered around him. "Whatever the name, the principle is the same." Five balls now flew in circles in front of him. "It's the manipulation of the physical world through the metaphysical energies present in all things." He pointed at the fence, marking his targets. The balls fired off like gunshots, flying past his pointed finger and slammed into the fencing, embedding themselves into it. "Pull one of the balls out."

The task was a simple one. Even a monkey would understand it. But only a mage would be capable of doing it. Dodger had received his first magic lesson from professional tailor Charles Pickens and so he was capable of manipulating the thick metal threads of the fencing.

Oliver approached the fencing and did just as Dodger thought he would. He grabbed the nearest ball and gave it a tug. The ball didn't budge. He tugged again, this time a little harder and nothing happened. He looked back and saw that his smug grin had turned into one of disapproval. A hint of embarrassment crept its way into Oliver's stomach. It was his first real task as an agent of Nightwatch and yet he was floundering.

He tried using both his hands. He tried pushing and pulling. His temper flared and he kicked the fence. But nothing worked. He felt like giving up. He repeated this process with all the other balls. He had so little experience with magic that he didn't understand what was going on nor had he noticed the state the balls were actually in. The balls were lodged more tightly into the fence than the fence was to the ground. Oliver believed the balls had merely been jammed into the holes of the fence and so only needed a similar show of force to free them. That was his first mistake and one a more knowledgeable individual would not make. The true test was not to remove the balls, but to understand how to remove them.

"I can't!" Oliver threw his hands up in a tantrum. "It's impossible."

"That is why you've never tapped into the finer points of your potential." Dodger mocked as he sauntered over. "Mana, ethos, sensus, corporis, animus, these are the foundations of magic and something you're going to have to learn." He pointed to one of the balls. "What do you see?"

"I see a ball stuck in the fence." He believed himself to be stating the obvious but he was still failing to see the truth in Dodger's test. The depth of the situation had yet to set in. He was still a child, ignorant of what people were actually capable of. Dodger never had this sort of mental block. He had started training when his eyes were still bright and ready to accept whatever absurdity he was told.

"Well, you're technically correct. But look closer." He grabbed his student by the back of the head and pointed to the seams. The virgule threads that once held the leather together had been deeply intertwined with the steel wiring of the fence. To force the ball out one would need to apply enough force to tear the ball apart. This was a level of strength not found in ordinary people and even if Oliver possessed that strength, freeing the ball in this manner would destroy it.

"That's...how?" Oliver's eyes lit up as he finally understood Dodger's lesson.

"Magic." He grabbed the ball. "If you don't know what you're looking for, you won't find it. Just like how you can't hit the ball without knowing that the ball is there." In an instant, the threads unraveled and he popped the ball out without any issue.

Now that Oliver's eyes were open he was ready to receive the tenant that served as the foundation of all forms of magic. Everything in the physical world consists of energies. Broadly these energies were referred to as mana. Mana came in many forms but the primary one used by mages was ethos. Ethos was present in all living things. Mages could use that ethos to manipulate the mana all around them and achieve all sorts of wondrous abilities.

"Everything?" Oliver pondered. That word as he took in his surroundings. "Like how atoms have energy."

"Figures a string bean like you would be a nerd. That's exactly the case. Knowing that much, makes the next step easier. If you know something intimately, you can use your ethos to dominate it."

"Wow." Oliver was at a loss for words. He thought that there would be runes or magic words or powerful artifacts or incantations. Of course, there were all of those things but they were all different flavors of the same principles that guided all forms of magic.

Dodger had lingered on his prior comment long enough. Oliver had a ton of mana. With it would come a powerful ethos. Looking him over Dodger made a very educated guess on why the boy had been kept away from this stuff for so long. If his potential were to be unlocked, his body couldn't hope to keep up. People of his inheritance were a rare sort and they often lived short lives. They often flew too close to the sun before they could even manifest a meager flame. And it would destroy them.

"Next, drop down and give me some pushups. Stronger the body, the stronger the spirit. Stronger the spirit, stronger the mana. When you're ready, we'll start to cover the basics and go out on patrols."

That was the first day of Dodger's training. Oliver would have to get used to the physical side of things if he was to prepare for the task ahead. For that same night a plot was set in motion that would threaten to engulf the entire city. As the sun began to set a man from Chicago approached a certain bar. The man's name was Briggs and while he may seem out of place with his fancy suit, he had an unflappable demeanor that made him look comfortable no matter where he might be sitting. He took his seat in a backroom and wasted no time placing his briefcase on the table. The man across from him was a total stranger but one who showed immense promise. Upon hearing who Briggs worked for and the part he would play, this thug for hire let out a laugh. A smoldering purple flame danced across his fingers as he lit himself a cigarette and agreed to the plot.

CHAPTER 5

The Tria-Ethos

Oliver was having a much easier time with his reading homework than his physical training. The more intensive his physical conditioning the more ill he felt. He had always described it as a burning pain in his stomach. He had tried to power through it to keep from disappointing Dodger. But the older boy was more astute than Oliver could have predicted. It hadn't taken him long to see Oliver's limits. Now his daily goal was to push those limits.

By Dodger's estimations it would take six-to-eight months for Oliver to get a grasp on his own powers. These things took time. They never came naturally, not even to the most talented of mages. Power was like a flame. Too much too quickly could leave a mage scorched and ruined. Not enough fuel and it would starve and die out. It was because of this training requirement that so few mages existed. Roughly ten-percent of Earth's population had the potential to become mages but only half of them even stuck with it long enough to grasp the tria-ethos.

The tria-ethos are the three schools of physical augmentation: sensus, corporis and animus. Anybody who hadn't at least grasped one of these augmentations had no chance in a fight against a mage. Most mages that make it in the world have grasped the whole tria-ethos. Doing so was the requirement to become an active member of The Celestial Order.

Sensus was Dodger's specialty. By tapping into this a mage will be able to see the cascading fields of mana that bind all things. Those who can see such truths can more easily manipulate it. It's the second sight that gives one perception far beyond what ordinary people can do.

Corporis was the most important for those who tend to be reckless. It was the specialty of Amelia Petrochilos and any other who wished to fight with physical strength. By tapping into this a barrier would manifest, granting the mage superhuman strength, speed and durability.

Animus was the specialty of Eliza Alcius and all those who wished to cast manifestations of their will across great distances. By tapping into this a mage's raw mana would be internalized, increasing its potency and becoming a weapon in its own right.

For each of the tria-ethos there were multiple levels dictated by naturally occurring abilities that could only manifest upon testing the limits of one's own abilities and understanding of the world around them. The abilities that dictated these levels numbered five for each ethos. No individual in all of recorded history had been able to make all fifteen abilities manifest. Mages tended to favor one of the tria-ethos and stuck with the lesser abilities of the other two.

Even with Oliver's great potential, he would likely only ever grasp twelve or thirteen of these abilities. That was only assuming he stuck with his training and kept pushing his limits without going overboard. All of which made for a delicate balancing act for anyone who wasn't already accustomed to such things. Oliver was feeling the pressure and had already manifested some doubt in his abilities. Especially after hearing how long it would take just to grasp the basics.

"If worse comes to worse, I can always just throw you off a building and see what happens." Dodger joked. He decided levity would benefit the anxious teen. He was probably the only agent under Sir Nightwatch that could relate to Oliver on this level. It made the older boy question just how far into the future the old man could see.

"Wait what?!" Oliver said.

"Just kidding ... mostly." Dodger chuckled.

"I am not okay with that."

"It worked for me."

Oliver's face turned red. Dodger could see the chemicals in his brain churning, trying to decipher where the instruction ended and the joke began. It didn't matter. What mattered was that Oliver took everything in stride. If he learned nothing else from Dodger, he needed to at least learn that.

"I don't know. It seems like it's so far off and if I even take a break I'll never reach it." Oliver lamented.

"Can't think like that. Or, well, the first part. Yeah, if you get too complacent you'll fall behind. Just like anything in your life. But you'll get there before you know it. The old man sees potential and so do I."

"Potential? Is it just because of my mother?" He asked.

"Well, you gotta understand that this stuff is genetic. Strong people have strong kids. But people with sensus ethos like me can see people's potential. In terms of magic, that's not some nebulous term, it's an actual quantifiable force. Now, living up to your potential is entirely up to you."

This begged another question and one Oliver had on his mind ever since he met Sir Nightwatch. It was difficult enough being a teenager in a new town. Now he had to deal with all of this.

"How do you balance this life with schoolwork?" Oliver asked with a sigh.

"Pfft. Funny that you think I care. It's all just a cover. And networking. But mostly cover."

"Networking?"

"You'll meet other mages in due time." Dodger said.

"There's other mages?"

"I guess a kid who spent so much time in the boonies wouldn't have run into very many mages. Word of advice, be eager to make acquaintances, hesitate to make friends. It'll make everything about your life a hell of a lot easier. Friends can just be extra baggage. Around the wrong people, it can be used as leverage against you. Acquaintances have all the benefits of friends while being useful in their own right. And more importantly, without the emotional investment, it hurts a lot less if something happens to them."

Oliver let the words sink in. Had he met Sir Nightwatch just one night earlier this would have been an easy lesson for him to take to heart. After all, he had already contemplated if he even wanted friends at this school. But it was too little too late for that. He had already met Rachel and her group. Even if he was determined to keep her at a distance it would have been difficult. He met Rachel first and the girl had put in the effort to befriend him. The thought of any of Dodger's warnings coming to fruition because of her was enough to make Oliver feel sick again. He needed to take his mind off it and so he asked another important question.

"Dodger, when do I start learning how to do the cool stuff?" Oliver asked.

"You have to walk before you can run." The older boy replied. "This isn't like the movies. One well placed fireball without the proper protection can be the death of you, no matter how much innate potential you might have. But...next time I go on patrol, you can sit back and watch."

It was a risk to be sure. Dodger knew he was gambling here. He merely wished to placate his comrade's insecurities in as safe a way as he could. It worked to lighten his mood. It can be hard to visualize what you can do without seeing someone else do it first. Once upon a time Sir Nightwatch had Dodger bear witness to some of his exploits. So in Dodger's mind, it wouldn't hurt for him to do the same. So long as they encountered a demon and not a real monster it should go smoothly. That was what Dodger thought at the very least.

CHAPTER 6

The First Flame

The month of September had only just begun. It was a mild night as a shadowy figure made his way down the street. There wasn't a soul in sight. Only the strong and the foolish would be out at this time of night in a neighborhood as rough as this. The southern parts of St. Louis were never the worst but still very much dangerous for those who failed to prepare for that which strides in darkness.

Glass and gravel littered the streets. Empty shot bottles laid strewn underfoot. Rundown apartment buildings watched over the lone figure. Anyone peering out their window would likely assume he was some junky or homeless vagabond. Even the flickering street lights did not provide enough illumination for anyone to notice how fresh his leather jacket was. He cast an imposing silhouette. He was tall and lanky and his hair was a shaggy mess of dark colors.

The only sound was that of his own footsteps and the occasional bark of a dog in the distance. The man was well accustomed to hiding his presence from the few who had the skills to stop him. Uneven as his steps were, they did not progress without purpose. He was approaching a familiar address but the reason behind his plan was not personal. He cared not for the resident. In fact, he couldn't even sense them inside. This was the home of a small hispanic lady named Mona Ramirez. She was a real-estate agent who owned several buildings throughout the area and the night-walker knew her because of the restaurant she owned.

Mona Ramirez seemed to be out of town. Even so the figure went around to the back alley. As purple flames danced along his fingers he wondered if this had anything to do with her restaurant. Not that it mattered to the professional criminal. He had been paid a handsome sum for the job he had here.

Gloveless fingers examined the back door. It was locked but no other security measure had been placed on the door. Whatever Mona Ramirez had done, she had done without any idea what was going to happen.

He burned away the screen in a flash and melted through the glass of the door. After letting himself in he made himself at home. He figured that if all things had mana, perhaps the house would enjoy its last moments being pleasant. The lights remained off for he wished not to alarm the neighbors before he was done. His suspicion about the house being empty was confirmed when he snuck into the bedroom for a peak.

Reliance on his sensus was paramount to his investigation. He had to navigate the cluttered home without making any noise that would alert the neighbors. Slowly but surely he examined every room, cabinet and closet looking for his quarry. He learned more about Mona Ramirez in that hour than he had the entire rest of his time interacting with her. Shelves were covered in figurines of various old cartoons. Pictures of her kids hung in frames along the walls. The only book in the whole house had been a Bible and it had a thin layer of dust on it.

It was in the basement that he finally found what he was looking for. It was a metal box about half the length of his arm. The container was locked but that was no problem for a man who knew magic. He opened it up, verifying the contents of the box. Inside was a bundle of contracts, the particulars of which held little interest to the man. He was looking for a specific set of documents. He had been given the invoice number by his employer so that he could accomplish his mission. He skimmed two of the documents, enough to verify that it was what he was after and get a firmer grasp on the situation.

It appeared Mona Ramirez was using her restaurant as a front to launder her property taxes. Whoever had tasked him with this job could reap the rewards of her labor right from under her nose. The documents were important. Without them Mona Ramirez would have to start any of her illegal activities from scratch. It would be a shame if they turned up missing after her home burned down.

With that, the burglar understood why he had been assigned to this job. He was the only one in St. Louis who was willing and able to carry out everything his employer desired. After he was done Mona Ramirez would run scared. She'd scramble to replace the documents and become thoroughly indebted to the one who salvaged them. If she told the police what exactly was stolen she would be incriminating herself as well. And any evidence this man may have left behind for police to track him down would all be burned away.

He dragged his hand across the wall, leaving a trail of embers in his wake. The fires he commanded were small and strategically placed so that they would grow and spread naturally until the entire residence was engorged in smoke and flame. By the time the fire burned bright enough for anyone to notice, he would be long gone.

He had done such a good job that the authorities had initially thought it was natural. They found that the lock had not been tampered with and had surmised that the flames started inside the house. With those two facts it would be easy for police to rule out both arson and theft. The fools couldn't be further from the truth. Mona Ramirez knew but she couldn't cooperate for her own sake. It would be another two months before a lone police officer, following a tip from a mysterious phone call, looked into this case once again and found the evidence that it had been arson. Upon that discovery it was time to bring Arch Knight Eliza Alcius on the case.

CHAPTER 7

Night of the Vampyr

S unday night in St. Louis was often quiet. Like any piece of urban sprawl, it had not entirely fallen asleep. There were still people cutting through the Gateway City on their way to more pressing destinations. The mild weather bore no ill will to the homeless that made themselves comfortable in whatever crevice was coziest. The pale moon watched over the old city, casting its reflection off the mighty Mississippi. Nights like this were perfect for a hunt.

The Rift between worlds was constantly monitored. The nexus of otherworldly energies ebbed and flowed like the rivers that carved their way through the continent. If anything were to breach the veil, it was up to those who hunted monsters to keep the people safe.

St. Louis, and most other major cities for that matter, had been built along these rifts for good reason. The rifts tended to follow rivers, mountains and tectonic plates. Any natural formation capable of altering the landscape in its path was surely home to a rift. Often these rifts were small, too small for any creature to get through. But in places where the rift widened, cities were built to better monitor them.

One tool at the disposal of monster hunters was a celestial compass. These had been designed by The Celestial Order hundreds of years ago to track anything that came through The Rift. Living creatures of the other worlds gave off a particular scent that the compass could sense in the same way a hound could sense the faintest traces of aroma in the air. Dodger had stolen one from Eliza Alcius some years earlier. On this night he allowed Oliver to hold the compass as he drove through the city streets.

The crystal disk fit nicely in Oliver's hand. It resembled the eye of an insect with its honeycomb structure. A green light blinked in its center representing their location. What Oliver had to keep an eye out for was any yellow dots forming on the edges of the crystal. Such lights would mark their prey.

Oliver called out one such light. Something had appeared from the other world and the agents of Nightwatch were on its trail. Eventually this led them to the old cathedral, one of the oldest structures in all of Missouri. Upon reaching such a close proximity, the celestial compass fulfilled its use. It was a vital tool, but one with a limit. The green and yellow dots were now on top of each other. This meant that the target was within fifty meters of the compass. It would be up to Dodger to track it down from there.

"Stay close to the car." Dodger said. "It's not a good neighborhood. Shout out if you see any movement on the compass. I'll hear."

"It's also probably safer for me to stay put." Oliver surmised.

"Eh, if things go south there's no telling how far it'll go." Dodger said as he jumped out of the car. "Considering that it stopped in a place like this, chances are it's demoran, and demorans can be reasoned with. But at the same time, they might also give me the slip."

There was one other tool that Dodger had at his disposal, and one that would even allow Oliver to hold his own in a pressing situation. In Dodger's glovebox was a gun. He had already instructed Oliver on how to use it. Until Oliver was able to harness his power, a gun would be the only weapon he could use.

Oliver examined the pistol for a few moments before shoving it into his jeans. Dodger parted ways with him and moved behind the cathedral. He looked for traces of his quarry all around the block. After disappearing behind one of the adjacent buildings he felt a sliver of silver rest on his shoulder.

"Haven't met many people who could get the drop on me." Dodger held his bat tightly. If he made the wrong move he risked injury before the fight could actually begin.

"I'm not here to fight." The voice was male and judging from his accent he had spent a lot of time in Missouri. Dodger didn't need to face forward to sense that the stranger was wearing a specialized stealth suit. Whoever this was, it wasn't who he was after.

"So, what's the story then?" Dodger asked.

"I'm not in the business of telling kids my business." The figure stood unmoving. Dodger tried using his own psychic prowess to pry into his captor's thoughts. It was a fruitless venture and one that put Dodger on edge. The man in black was equipped to deal with all sorts of mages. He had his own mission and was hoping to keep blood off his blade for the night.

"You know there's a monster nearby." Dodger said. "If you're not here to fight me then maybe we could work together."

"Is that what you think?"

A piercing shriek echoed from inside the cathedral. The man in black made no motion and betrayed no thought. Green flames danced across Dodger's body. He could never see very far into the future but one need not have a strong sensus to know that this was going to get worse.

Oliver was drawn to this same shriek. For a moment he contemplated leaving things to Dodger. But after a second shriek he was called to action. The sound that came from the cathedral drew him in like a moth to a flame. The boy's hands were shaking. Sweat poured from his brow as he slowly opened the cathedral door. He was expecting resistance but the door gave way at the slightest push.

The lights were out but there were a few candles lit around the building. The faint light gave the cathedral an eerie glow. The ceilings were tall, reaching for the heavens. But aside from the candles, which were nearing the end of their wicks, there wasn't anything out of the ordinary. It was well furnished. On the inside, it looked far newer than the outside ever could.

A third shriek urged Oliver past the church altar where he located the door that went up to the bell tower. This part of the church was not as well maintained.With modern technology, the need to manually ring the bell had been replaced with automatic ringers. And with it, less need to maintain the staircase heading up the tower.

The stairs creaked as the boy made his way to the top. He was too nervous to even speak up. With each step he had to rationalize this fit of bravery. Dodger was surely close by. Maybe Dodger was already there. Maybe it was nothing. With each step Oliver took his thoughts grew darker and darker. What if it was something bad? What if Dodger was already dead? The dread was enough to dry the boy's throat.

When he reached as far as the steps would take him he saw a figure hunched over in the corner. Its back was bare and leathery. A row of small scutes ran along its spine in pairs. Its arms were proportionally large and were covering its face. The lower half looked slightly more human. It wore pants but its feet were bedecked in talons like a hawk.

"Hello?" Oliver said, remembering that demorans could be reasoned with. Bartleby had been a demoran and looked far more monstrous than this creature. The thought of this thing having sentience was the only source of hope left in Oliver's mind.

The monster twitched. It looked dead into the eyes of its new prey with four oval red eyes that made the boy's blood run cold. Its head continued to twitch back and forth with each unnatural movement and drool ran down its spider-like maw. The strands of saliva mixed with blood, dripping onto the stone and created small plumes of hissing smoke. The source of the blood was the mangled corpse of a large bat it clutched within its claws.

This creature was a vampyr, a parasitic monster that could change its appearance based on what it ate. Naturally they looked like hairy spiders with four limbs. This one had already devoured many insects, a hawk, numerous snakes and a human before ripping the bat to shreds. Usually that would be plenty of sustenance to satisfy a vampyr but this one was driven by an insatiable hunger that no amount of blood would satisfy.

Oliver slowly raised his gun. The hunk of metal felt heavy in his hands. His feet hit the wall and his back faced the opening in the bell tower. The creature's next shriek was enough to rupture Oliver's ears. And then it was right in front of him. Panicked finger pulled the trigger. The first bullet whizzed past its shoulders and the next pierced its chest. Before the third bullet could fly, one claw grabbed his shoulder and the other reached for his head. The gun fell from his hand as he instinctively caught that arm. Oliver's left hand swung wildly at the monster's head. He was trying to blind it and keep its twitching mandibles as far away as possible.

Oliver was hyperventilating. He could feel the creature overpowering him. Muscles weeped for extra strength. They began to burn and glow as he held the monster off for precious seconds. Its jaws unhinged and a pincer extended out towards the boy. Oliver struggled to keep it at bay and dug his pathetic excuse for nails into its eyes. The attempt was not without merit. Oliver's thumb forced its way into one of the monster's eyes. The pupil popped and pussed as Oliver pushed forward.

In its agitation, it changed tactics. It took the claw that had clung to Oliver's shoulder and slapped him in the chest. Oliver's grip tightened around the monster's face and hand enough to where they both tumbled out of the bell tower and down towards the yard below. The creature's back miraculously sprouted bat-like wings and halted its descent. Oliver lost his grip and slipped, saved only by his ability to clutch onto its ankle.

The vampyr kicked its leg up. Oliver's grip slipped and he again found himself in its claws. This time, the burning sensation of his muscles was much brighter. It was burning with the same golden glow that had accompanied the single punch he threw at Bartleby.

That glow coincided with two things. The first was the man in black looking up to the sky to see what had tumbled out of the bell tower. This momentary lapse in attention was enough for Dodger to strike the man. The second was a dextrous pale feminine hand spinning a dial to distort the world the same way it had been when Sir Nightwatch battled Bartleby. This was Oliver's second time in what was known as Reflected Sphere. This was where mages did battle without causing harm to any civilian or damage to any structure.

The creature shrieked and spun around. Oliver could no longer hear anything. His ears were damaged to the point where he could only feel the noise and the blood running down his cheeks. The creature had thrown him away like a bag of garbage. He flew through the air, feeling the wind pass through his ruptured ear drums. He closed his eyes, awaiting the darkness that awaited him for when he hit the ground. That darkness never came. Basal Knight Amelia Petrochilos had snatched him out from the jaws of certain death.

"Got'cha." Waves of scarlet surrounded Oliver. When they landed on a nearby building she shoved him to the ground and raised a bronze shield. She was ready to defend the monster's would-be victim. She was fully clothed in the armor of the amazonians who had raised her. She wore brown combat boots and black leggings leading up to a red half skirt. Her shins and chest were covered in bronze armor that matched her shield. Her red hair was pulled back into a ponytail by a circlet that matched her armor.

With the boy saved, the knight moved on to the next stage of her mission. She drew her sword. Her blade had been forged in the fires of Greece's Methana Volcano by a mage who specialized in green flame. The forger whose name was engraved along its bronze hilt had made a dozen swords like it. He had divided his very soul into pieces, imbuing his prized creations with a flame that would never be extinguished. Even someone who had never learned the ways of magic could summon a meager flame. In the hands of an experienced knight of The Celestial Order, it could summon an emerald inferno. Each enchanted weapon had a different name and this one went by Kapselimeno Donti–The Scorched Fang.

The blade lived up to its name as the flesh of the vampyr was scorched. Driven by instinct it cowered from the flames. Had this been a mere wildfire the monster could have escaped to safety. Instead the amazon sent another wave of flames to strike it across the chest. Then, an ivory tether pierced the monster's charred flesh. This manifestation of mana had been summoned by the same pale hand that had summoned the Reflected Sphere. With her target restrained, the knight rocketed up to the roof and pierced the monster's shoulder. Everything from the shoulder down to the tips of its clawed hand expanded and popped like a balloon. The pressure required for such a feat generated enough heat to vaporize the vampyr's acidic blood.

This was the work of Arch Knight Eliza Alcius. Her outfit was white with blue trimmings on the chest, sleeves and collar. Her hair was platinum blonde, long and tied back with a ponytail. There was an elegance to her as she raised her rapier in her left hand, directing its sharp tip towards the vampyr. This rapier was a weapon more notorious than Amelia's sword. The width of the blade was etched with ancient nordic runes heralding the wind, the moon and the tides. Its name was Manegennebore–The Moon Piercer.

Eliza struck a regal and elegant figure. Even facing something as vile as a vampyr didn't heed her resolve in the slightest. But underneath that visage of cold heroic professionalism was an intense fire in her eyes. All of this made her the most beautiful woman in Oliver's eyes.

She lunged for the creature again and it managed to hover around her stab with its one remaining wing. Snakes sprouted from the wound and snapped at the snowy knight. She created a pure white forcefield that took the brunt of the attacks. A few snake appendages circled around the shield, forcing her to do a series of handsprings to get out of their reach without getting hit. Her sensus, though not as developed as Dodger's, was more than enough to track each simultaneous attack.

With a flick of her wrist, she summoned a trail of ice that extended from her to the creature. The attack ran up the monster's leg, trapping it. Its next move forced it to break its frozen leg off. In its place a human foot sprouted.

It sprayed acid at the platinum princess and tried limping away. But then a baseball encased in green flame pelted it in its head, dropping the creature to the ground. The man in black had abandoned the fight when Eliza showed up, allowing Dodger to aid in the fight. He dropped down on the vampyr's head and kicked off its chest. When he landed on his feet he was next to Amelia and Oliver.

"Good evening Red." Dodger said.

"Is this your doing?" She asked. Dodger sneered mockingly.

"We have this under control!" Eliza's temper flared whenever Dodger intervened. This temper ran hotter than ever after seeing the perilous situation Oliver had been in.

"That thing must have eaten a hydra. You're going to have to burn it to death!" Dodger shouted back.

"Don't tell me what to do!" She yelled back. She didn't need his advice. She knew full well what she was up against. The presence of a hydra within explained why it was able to replace lost limbs with other creatures it had eaten. The flames she summoned were as blue as her eyes. She planned to incinerate the creature as quickly as possible.

Dodger had a slightly different plan. He had a single sulfuric lure he knew would attract the vampyr. It smelled of a slumbering demoran. The vampyr would instinctively fly headlong towards the lure in pursuit of more power. That would give Dodger and Amelia the chance to finish it off.

"You and I both like to play with fire." Dodger said as he lit the bait. "We'll take this ugly son of a bitch down together."

The creature flew towards the stick. Dodger's body began to light up as he held his bat with both hands. He raised it high above his head.

He focused on his own corporis. His body grew slightly with each heart-beat. He was ready to go all out with this one attack. Then, just before the monster was in range, the roof turned into spikes piercing the monster across its body. Eliza had molded the rooftop to suit her will and stabbed the vampyr through until it was pinned to the roof. Through the unique power of her blade the beast's body expanded and tore itself to ribbons on the spikes. Amelia followed her partner's strike with a scorching wave of her sword.

The monster was all but dead. Its original parasitic form detached itself from the smoldering corpse and tried scurrying away. Dodger was the only one who could see through the flames well enough to see the creature's desperate escape. But instead of warning anyone, he wished to kill it himself.

"I guess y'all don't get to see my little parlor trick tonight." Dodger said.

"I told you we had this under control!" Eliza shouted. Dodger smirked as he took a few more steps right where the vampyr parasite was scurrying. With a single stomp he crushed what little life it had left.

"Thanks for the assist." Dodger said as he snapped his fingers, causing the crushed creature to combust and die.

"Typical, having us ladies do all the work." Eliza spun the dial on her Reflected Sphere Generator. The world returned to as it had been. The changes Eliza had made to the roof scattered into dust. The smears of blood left by the vampyr evaporated. And the night was calm once again. "Are you even a real man?" As she continued to chastise Dodger for bringing an untrained kid on a hunt Amelia saw to said child's wounds. Healing was something neither Amelia nor Eliza were well-versed in but they had both learned basic first aid techniques while at the mage academy. It was well enough for Oliver's ears to be repaired and any other flesh wounds to close. As soon as he was able to hear properly, Amelia made her introduction.

"And what in the blazes are you doing bringing a guy like that here with you!" Eliza's voice cut the introductions short.

"Well excuse me Princess." Dodger defended. "We just happened to be in the area. It's not like I was looking for trouble. But when the compass started pinging I decided to act."

"Yeah right!" She argued back. "Even if I believed that, it only proves my point that you are a dolt and a delinquent and have no business chasing monsters! It is my job to protect the people in this city and you have a habit of making things worse!"

"Excuse me!" Oliver raised his hand. "But who are you?" Oliver had seen Amelia in passing at school but Eliza's was a face he had only ever seen from a distance before.

"Ah yes. Princess, Red, meet my protege Oliver Turner. Oliver, meet,"

"Lady Eliza Alcius. Arch Knight of The Celestial Order. Daughter of Paladin Sir Henry Alcius of America and Dame Anne Rosen-Alcius of Denmark. Heir to the,"

"This could take a while." Dodger interrupted by whispering to his partner.

"I guess it's not important." Eliza was flustered to the point of her face taking a slight red tint. "This is my partner and shield bearer, Amelia Petrochilos."

"Hello again." Amelia waved.

"She too is a celestial knight." Eliza continued.

"Though I'm just a basal knight, not an arch knight like Eliza." Amelia added.

"Think of them more like competition." Dodger said. "We don't see eye to eye."

"You're the scum of the earth!" Eliza sneered.

"Do they do this often?" Oliver asked Amelia.

"You have no idea." She responded.

"At least we have the intelligence to train people before bringing them out on hunts." Eliza said.

"The compass said it was a demoran. I didn't think anything of it." Dodger said.

"Oh what else is new!" She threw her hands into the air. "Can't think, can't properly behave, I knew you were a dolt but I didn't realize you were that incompetent."

"I was just following the compass."

"The compass you stole from me!" Eliza got in his face. "And even if it was a demon and not a vampyr you still shouldn't bring a novice along!"

"Vampire?" Oliver asked.

"No, a vampyr, there's a difference." Amelia said. "Vampires are a class of demons. Vampyrs are parasitic monsters that take on the body parts and abilities of whatever they eat. And that one was the nastiest I've ever seen."

"We're getting nowhere with this." Eliza turned to face the novice. "Amelia, we're leaving. And Oliver, do yourself a favor and stay away from Dodger. He'll only cause you trouble."

"The Celestial Order is always looking for recruits." Amelia smiled.

"Don't listen to them." Dodger said. "You'll be fine. Now let's get out of here and get you back home."

Dodger didn't tell anyone about the man that had held him up. Instead he filed it away in the back of his mind. Only a few people in the country could afford a stealth suit of that quality. He would inform Sir Nightwatch alone about that detail. As the two groups parted ways the man in black watched from one of the adjacent rooftops.

"Two more mages than we originally thought." The man said into his headpiece. He nodded as he received a response from his boss. "Very well, just let me know when the other specimens arrive."

CHAPTER 8

The Second Flame

The same night as the altercation with the vampyr, the arsonist was fulfilling his second job. He had been given specific instructions once again but this time he needn't worry about entering the house. He was nervous about committing any acts in Shadowbrooke. He knew of three mages who all lived nearby who could be capable of stopping him.

He had been assured by his employer that they would be luring any monster hunters away from Shadowbrooke. The arsonist didn't ask any further. The man who hired him had already proven to be capable of controlling the situation and so he trusted him and his people to do their job.

The house where they would light their second flame was the residence of Donovan Brown. He was the favored candidate in the upcoming mayoral race. He had also appeared on one of the many notes stolen from the house of Mona Ramirez. She was the one who sold the house to this young up and coming politician.

The most important thing for this job was to make it look like a hate crime. Donovan Brown was a black man and one who fought for social justice. He ran on a platform of police reform and securing federal funds to help the homeless. He was sometimes divisive in his language which would make this act of terror much more believable. The media was always eager to find hatred where there was none. This arsonist had no ill will towards Donovan Brown. In fact, had he lived in Shadowbrooke he would vote for the man. But in order to complete this job, the man's belongings had to burn.

Per his employer's instructions, he made sure to conceal his identity before walking in view of the camera. He needed there to be a mystery as to his identity but not to his race. He concealed any distinguishing feature but left parts of his pale skin exposed. He then tossed a rope tied in a noose over the nearest tree.

Donovan Brown and his family were still out at a fundraiser. The arsonist had plenty of time to contemplate how best to burn down the house. He considered himself something of an artist. He could destroy the building in an instant if he wanted to. But few things captivated him more than a natural flame. Spreading the fire through more natural means also suited their schemes and kept The Celestial Order from getting involved with the case for a little longer. He decided on a baseball. He quickly fashioned a molotov baseball and hurled it through the window. As he did he couldn't help but grin as he remembered a kid he once tried to take under his wing.

As far as any spying cameras could detect this was where it ended. The flame would burn for a few minutes before authorities would arrive to put out the fire. That was fine for their true motive was to scare Donovan Brown but not in the way the media would claim. This wasn't a threat to his life. At least it wasn't yet. This was a show of force. Whoever employed the arsonist wanted Donovan Brown on his team.

He was once again satisfied with his work and vanished before any emergency responders could arrive. The very next night the whole country would hear about this story from one of the most famous and passionate TV News personalities.

Damien Crow had a whole segment on what he described as: "A vile and racist hate crime meant to terrify any black man who wished to stand up to the systemic problems of middle America." He invited Donovan Brown onto his show to wax poetic about all the things he had lost and how thankful he was that he and his family were safe. Meanwhile the police were baffled that the flame spread so quickly. Community leaders organized rallies on behalf of Donovan Brown. Any political group that could use this event to preach from their pulpit did so. There were only three people who had glimpsed through this turn of events.

The first was Eliza Alcius who instantly grew suspicious at the timing of this crime. She notified her superiors that she planned to allocate more time to patrolling Shadowbrooke. The baseball present at the crime scene also made her suspicious of Dodger, and by extension Oliver.

The second was Dodger. He had already suspected there was more to the vampyr than a mere monster. Vampyrs rarely if ever got that powerful. He suspected that it had been raised, altered and fed by someone connected to the man in the stealth suit. Eliza did not yet know of this man and even she was suspicious of how strong the vampyr had been.

The third was Sir Nightwatch. His network of agents had already detected some detestable players making a move on St. Louis. He was skeptical of any news that came out of the Gateway City that did not come directly from the mouth of Dodger. If this persisted, he may need to act on his own to give his agents the push they needed to quell this flame before it engulfed the city.

CHAPTER 9

A Few Thoughts on Current Happenings

One thing they never tell you is how much paperwork is involved for all those who fight against criminals. Eliza Alcius was filling out such paperwork regarding the attack on the vampyr. It was far too powerful to be a normal naturally occurring threat. She suspected it was raised by humans and if that was the case she would need to request a formal inquisition.

Arch knights were given far more autonomy than other members of their ranks. She rarely had to take direct orders from anyone. She was allowed to hunt monsters and defend civilians at her own discretion. Eliza never took full advantage of that autonomy. She always made herself available to the county sheriff and all the police precincts within the territory she had been given.

Working with local authorities was part of The Celestial Order's purview. They were the largest organization of mages in the world and one of the only ones officially sanctioned by various governments. Every nation in Europe, both Americas and Australia heavily relied on The Celestial Order to deal with other worldly threats. This was the opposite of Nightwatch. Nightwatch was unsanctioned, knowledge of their existence was not public. Only members of The Celestial Order's Grand Council and a few select high ranking members were privy to that information.

Eliza herself had never heard of Nightwatch. As far as she was aware Dodger was a lone wolf who refused to work with anyone up until this point. Eliza was intuitive enough to see some of Oliver's potential. It rivaled any she had seen before. But potential alone does not make a mage. She struggled to wrap her head around how Dodger could be so foolish.

She had also been suspicious of him for years. Ever since they first met she had kept an eye on him, waiting for the moment he slips up. If he ever stepped out of line or broke the law, she would execute him herself.

As she composed her letter to her superiors she was interrupted by her servant. Viggo Pendersen was a small, balding man who had attended one of The Celestial Order's academies. He had failed to join the active ranks and as both punishment of this failure and as a reward for the effort and devotion he had shown, he was hired by the Rosen noble family. The Rosens were one of the twelve founding families of The Celestial Order. The current head of the family was Anne Rosen, Eliza's mother. Viggo had tended to Eliza her entire life and maintained the house where Eliza and Amelia both lived. He had taken to mager work to help pay the living expenses but most of their finances were taken care of by The Celestial Order.

"I made tea, Ms. Eliza." Viggo offered a small cup and pot situated on a silver tray. Eliza made no vocal response nor did she make eye contact. She merely pointed to the spot on her desk where she wished for him to place the tray. "If I may, try not to stay up too late." Despite having lived in America for several years his Danish accent was far thicker than Eliza's. "Ms. Amelia has already turned in for the night."

"I won't be too much longer so stop worrying about me." Eliza said.

"I don't think that's possible." He said as he gently shut the door.

Eliza didn't mind school but she also had little interest in it. She attended mostly because music was one thing she genuinely loved and her high school band class was the only time she had to play her flute. As a member of The Celestial Order she had received a private education from an early age, a more formal education at the academy, and only started attending public school when she was stationed in St. Louis.

Most people in The Celestial Order only worked to protect the world part time. The rest of their time was spent at regular jobs living normal lives. Eliza had no such luxury nor was she envious of people who did. Her father descended from German nobility and owned a real-estate business in New York. Her mother descended from Danish nobility and they had always been involved with The Celestial Order. Never once did someone who carried that heritage waiver in their duty to the Order. Eliza was no exception. She was a staunch fundamentalist with a dream to become the first ever woman to hold the highest position within the knight branch of The Celestial Order. Her ultimate dream was to one day become the Grand Priest. St. Louis was just a stepping stone.

Nightwatch, and by extension Dodger, didn't have the same revenue streams The Celestial Order did. Sir Nightwatch had saved many wealthy socialites in his time. Those individuals privately donated money to Sir Nightwatch in good faith. There was also the suit shop where one could find Charles Pickens working for a considerable sum that then went to pay the expenses of a few agents. Other than Dodger and a handful of other mages all the agents had their own jobs and lives and acted more as informants than actual servants. All of them would act on Sir Nightwatch's orders if the time called for it.

So to do his job as a monster hunter and private mage investigator, Dodger had to keep his eyes on the paper. He read every single local paper and watched the evening news every day, looking for anything suspicious. By the middle of September he had noticed some strange details about the series of fires that had sprung up across the St. Louis area. The police hadn't been worrying about them since nobody had died but that alone was suspicious to Dodger.

With this level of skepticism he began digging a little deeper and found one arson that may be connected. It had gone under reported. Damien Crow had no way of turning its details into sensational news and so nobody outside the area would ever know about it. Meanwhile the police would never make the connection for one simple fact, someone had died.

That certain someone was Salma Robles. She wasn't anyone important in the public eye. The only connection she had to the other two was that she had been a manager at the restaurant owned by Mona Ramirez. Dodger had visited the restaurant a few times but never particularly liked it. Their food tended to be overcooked and it didn't help that she had once employed a couple street punks who liked to burn more than just food.

Upon making this connection Dodger made his way to the restaurant and inquired about those employees. It turns out all three of these delinquents lost their jobs earlier that same year. That gave the gang motive to burn down the home of Salma Robles and perhaps even Mona Ramirez. The one that didn't fit the profile was Donovan Brown. Political targets were usually out of this gang's budget. But if someone had heard about their prior exploits and hired them to intimidate a politician, they'd take the money and do the job with few questions asked.

This gang was The Hellfire Brats. Dodger had once infiltrated their gang as part of his first job in St. Louis. It didn't go well. He wasn't able to play along with their games and ended up fighting their leader. Dodger lost but not without giving the leader a nasty burn scar on his chin and neck. Sebastian Crane was still the leader of the gang as far as Dodger knew. Sebastian was savvy enough to do this sort of work without ever once catching the attention of The Celestial Order. That was doubly impressive since he and his two best friends were all demorans. Because of this secretive acumen only a demoran or a similarly shrewd criminal could get close to them.

They never revealed their true demoran forms. They had lived among humans long enough to lose their original scent. They would not be so easily located by a celestial compass or a piece of bait. Even when Dodger had infiltrated the group, he had done so accidentally. Sebastian Crane had found a then fifteen-year-old Dodger wandering the streets of St. Louis looking for a fight. Sebastian, who had been five years older than Dodger, thought he had found a kindred spirit but couldn't have been more mistaken.

Dodger hadn't gone after them since then. He found them mostly harmless and had little faith that he could beat any one of them, let alone all three of them in a fight. But if The Hellfire Brats were behind this recent string of arsons Dodger would have to confront them regardless of his chances and hope for the best. He just hoped that Oliver could keep up.

CHAPTER 10

Practice and Proposal

September was coming to a close and Oliver was feeling anxious. He had been given drills to run through every day while Dodger looked into other matters. He felt like he was being left behind even though he had yet to catch up in the slightest.

In his desperation he had turned to the only other mages he knew. After their fateful rooftop meeting Oliver and Eliza had become increasingly aware of each other's presence. Oliver asked Eliza for help and she turned him down. She had neither the time nor the patience to train a novice.

Amelia had been kinder. She at least gave him some tips on how to condition his body. Dodger–compared to the other mages at the school–had a low mana level. He had never had to worry about his body keeping up with the energy he used for his magic. Eliza and Amelia did have to worry about such things and Oliver would have to heed such drawbacks even more than them.

Luckily Amelia wasn't the only one in the life of Oliver Turner who was willing to push from that direction. Oliver had ignored Rachel Rune's invitation to join the track team but he had still found himself within the athlete's social circle. Rachel had volunteered Oliver to be her new jogging partner as a response to his wishes to get in better shape. Unlike the celestial knights and Nightwatch's most trusted agent, Rachel had plenty of time for the fledgling.

Every time they ran together Rachel would stay right next to him. Every time he had to catch his breath, she was there to pat him on the back. By the start of October, Oliver was in better shape than he ever had been. Albeit he was still lagging far behind the ones he aspired to catch up to. Each day he would look into the mirror unsatisfied with his progress. And each day a worried expression would cross Rachel's face for but a fleeting moment. Unbeknownst to the fledgling, Rachel knew all too well what he was going through.

At night Oliver's dreams were taken hostage by the vampyr. There had been a few times early in his life where his illness nearly took him. Alas for those he had been barely cognizant. The vampyr was a situation where he had been very much conscious and therefore it had a far stronger effect than any fever.

His only respite was the waking world. Once there the vampyr could no longer cling to his throat. Instead he had to enjoy the more meager challenges of student life. He would spend those hours pretending to be a normal student once again. When the bell rang to relieve him of these duties he would either go jogging with Rachel or head to the ballpark to see if he was able to do magic yet.

One day he found himself just staring off into the clouds wondering how much longer it was going to take. He felt like a fish trapped in a bowl. He could see the outside world from behind the glass and all he could do was wave his little fin at that which lay beyond him.

"You're not going to go anywhere standing in place like that." The glass of his bowl cracked as Amelia arrived with some training equipment of her own. Her clothes were far sportier than any Oliver had seen her in before. At school, she liked wearing skirts and baggy sweaters. In combat, she liked wearing armor. This was the first time Oliver had seen her in red jogging pants and a black tank top.

"What are you doing here?" Oliver asked.

"This place is the ideal training ground. I come here to do some practice for a few minutes on the rare day where my schedule allows me."

"Really?" Oliver's own lack of confidence led him down a path where he couldn't help but compare himself unfavorably to others. Here he was, mere feet away from someone who had reached full knighthood at twelve years old whereas he was fifteen and couldn't even do the basics.

"When I was little, my mom told me that if I want to get really good at something, I have to do it for fifteen minutes every day for an entire year. A year of that, actually gets you in the habit. And I've been doing it ever since." She took a moment to let the words of inspiration soak into Oliver's psyche before she brought up a separate order of business. "Don't let Eliza's callousness get you down."

"Did she tell you anything?"

"She mentioned you in her recent report." Amelia held her shield aloft as she began a practice drill of her own. She used telekinesis to spin her shield in the air like an alien ship. It spun faster and faster but never wobbled on its axis. Such a technique looked simple but keeping a bout of telekinesis running that smoothly for that long took a massive amount of training. "I'm sure Dodger has already told you that you can't force these sorts of things any more than you can force a child to learn how to swim."

"Yeah." That one immutable fact was both the source of Oliver's grief and his only solace in these depressing times.

"Well, sometimes the best way to take that first step is throwing you into the pool." Amelia said. "I think that's why Dodger wanted you to experience combat. I'm not like Eliza. I know better than to underestimate his cleverness. Now, when you struggled against the vampyr, what do you remember feeling?"

Oliver thought back to that night again. Amelia leaned in attentively as he described every sensation he could remember. He even recalled that it hadn't been the first time he felt that burning golden sensation.

"That." Amelia clapped. "Remember that feeling burning inside you. That is the spark that can create a powerful mage." She hoisted him up by the shoulder until he was standing straight. "Take a deep breath and close your eyes."

"Sure thing." He did as she asked and tried to remember that feeling. The only feeling that hit him though was her fingers ramming into his guts. Air burst from his lungs and suddenly he saw everything that happened that night like it was in fast-forward.

"Yep, you have a lot of mana." Amelia said.

"Warn me next time." Oliver grunted as he rubbed his stomach.

"In order to graduate from any mage academy, you have to show some proficiency in all three of the tria-ethos. But everyone is going to unlock one of them first, and the one they manifest first determines a lot about how they should train and what schools of magecraft they should look into."

"So, which one am I going to unlock first? Or is it too early to tell?"

"Unlock isn't really the best term. Develop actually fits more. And with that glowing light and the burning sensation it sounds like animus ethos."

"That's the one that shoots beams right?"

"Well it's far more versatile than that. It also happens to be the ethos that Eliza is strongest in. She actually has a level three animus. Not that the levels determine your power. It's just a declaration to how well you've developed that ethos to add to your arsenal."

"That doesn't help my predicament."

"Even a prodigy like Eliza used to be a novice." Amelia winked. "Now, she might not agree, but I think there's a potentially good ally in you."

"You do?"

"Dodger is a waste of talent if you ask me."

"Dodger is also standing right here rolling his eyes." Both of their attention was drawn to the new addition to this scene. It had been so long since Dodger had been able to join Oliver that the younger boy was not expecting his arrival. Amelia didn't take too kindly to his interruption. She gave him quite a nasty glare as she continued.

"But you have to have talent to waste it." She said "And as far as I've seen, he has extremely good eyes." She turned her gaze back to the younger novice and dropped her voice down to a whisper. "I'm just interested in seeing what it is he saw in you. And...you didn't hear this from me...but Eliza is curious about that too."

"So Red, what are you doing here?" Dodger asked.

"Well, I was just working on my telekinesis." Amelia said as she continued moving her shield through the air.

"Fancy that, I was actually going to teach Oliver that move." Dodger said.

"Oh, this early on? You think he's going to develop his animus first and be a caster." Amelia was playing dumb for her own amusement but Dodger had been watching long enough to pick up on that.

"If you came to that conclusion after jamming your fingers into his guts, then of course I came to that conclusion a while ago." Dodger said.

"Okay, now that we're on the same page how does telekinesis work?" Oliver inserted himself into the conversation and inserted himself between the two mages.

"This would be so much simpler if you just had your sensus like me." Dodger said.

"Now is that any way to talk to your student?" Amelia took on a mocking tone. "Go on, Mr. Dodger, explain it." Amelia said.

"Well, telekinesis is the simplest way to extend your will onto the world. You extend your energy out like a hand, or hands in my case." He demonstrated by levitating three baseballs from the bucket and spinning them on their axis while they rotated around his head. "The better you get, the heavier the weight you can carry, the more individual items you can carry and the finer the movements you can manage."

He added another baseball to the rotation. Then he added a fifth while he started showing off by juggling. Each ball he tossed was either added to the rotation or was sucked directly into his hand after finishing its ascent. But then one of the balls leapt from the air and slammed into Amelia's waiting hand.

"And like any technique, the more you spread yourself thin the easier it is for someone to use it against you." Amelia said. "Telekinesis is simple and easy to learn. So easy in fact, that it's impossible to master because no matter how powerful you are, make a mistake and someone will take advantage of it. That's why there's only a few people in The Celestial Order that hyper-specialize in telekinesis."

"You don't need to worry about that though." Dodger said. All the balls around his head dropped as he ripped the one out of Amelia's hand without taking a step. "This is just a way to help unlock your animus. Projecting your will is one of the fundamental building blocks of all spellcraft and your animus is your will weaponized through your mana." He launched the ball high into the air and fired a beam of green energy from his finger. The ball was perfectly pierced by the mana ray and was then guided onto his finger with telekinesis.

"Right now Eliza is strong enough to vaporize that whole bucket of balls in an instant." Amelia said.

"That would be a waste." Dodger said as he tossed the ball to Oliver. "Focus on the hole I made. Convince the ball to spin on that axis. Once you overcome that hurdle, getting it to move freely will come easy."

"He's right about that." Amelia said. "The first step is by far the most difficult for anyone wishing to become a mage."

"You know Red, you don't have to affirm or undermine every single thing I say."

"I just want to help Oliver get stronger. It'll be annoying if I have to keep saving him."

"That's the kind of thing Eliza would say. Did she put you up to this?"

"Just because I share her sentiments doesn't mean I'm just following orders. She doesn't know that I'm here right now. I decided all on my own that it'll help Oliver more if he had help from someone with a more formal education."

"We're going to the same school already." Dodger said as he put his hands behind his head.

"Was that an attempt at a joke?"

"Not really."

"I mean, I went to one of the most prestigious mage academies in the world. Who did you learn it from? Come to think of it, you've never told me."

"Just consider me self-taught." Dodger lied as naturally as he levitated baseballs.

"I think our dear Oliver should get the best training he can under the circumstances." Amelia said as she stood behind the small boy.

"I would appreciate all the help I can get." Oliver said. "If we're going to be meeting up a lot I'd rather be on good terms with them."

"I feel the same way." Amelia said.

"I do have to ask, why are you so eager to help me? Is it just because of my potential?" Oliver asked.

"I just like helping everyone who needs it. Eliza does too when she can get the stick out of her ass. Her ambitions pressure her to keep her distance from civilians. But like I said, don't let it get you down. She's really a sweet girl beneath all the angst and formalities."

"Anyway, we should let Oliver make a few attempts before he heads home." Dodger said.

The truth was he had found the breakthrough he was looking for. He was hot on the trail of the nefarious trio he suspected to be at the heart of the recent string of arsons. Even if they weren't directly involved it was very likely they would know something. Call it pride or call it foolish but Dodger wanted to track this lead and crack the case before Eliza got a single sniff of the sulfur and ash.

CHAPTER 11

The Hellfire Club

If you ever step into a little bar in downtown St. Louis and see drab walls lit entirely with candles that never seem to go out, then know that you are in the temporary location of The Hellfire Club. The gang tends to move around. It makes them difficult to find for anyone not looking for them, and even harder to track for anyone who is. This knowledge is something Dodger had that Eliza didn't. While the celestial knights have good relationships with the police and the politicians, Dodger had connections in the mold riddled underbelly of the urban streets.

He knew a couple bartenders downtown. Most of them owed him favors for one reason or another. He had told them to keep an eye out for Sebastian Crane and his little group of pyros. Less than a week later, he got a hit from one of these bartenders, a bosnian fellow named Lampi, claiming that Sebastian had set up shop in his bar.

Lampi's was secluded. It only had a little sign on the door and was between several bright shops. It was the perfect place for a demoran thug to hang out. For any normal highschooler, getting in provided a small challenge. Only people over the age of twenty-one were allowed to enter. But Dodger was no ordinary highschooler. For someone like him it wasn't an issue. Just a little alteration to his and Oliver's IDs and they let the pair in with no problem. Once inside, Lampi would cover for them per his agreement with the agent of Nightwatch. There was the obvious caveat that neither of them were allowed to drink anything harder than cherry cola.

There was a pool game and a darts competition going on in one corner of the smoky room. The rest of the patrons were smoking and drinking and being generally jolly. Oliver was so out of place he was starting to draw attention to himself just by trying to conceal his presence. This kind of bar was a place for extraverts to have fun, not for people to hide away or drown their sorrows. That's another thing that made it an unorthodox hideout for anyone hiding away from the prying eyes of The Celestial Order.

Dodger had to play up the charm double for the both of them just to keep anyone from asking Oliver more questions than he was ready to answer. Every moderately attractive girl got a wink and a nod. Every biker got sized up. Every slobbering drunk got a chuckle. To them, Dodger looked like a swinger taking a friend out for a drink he's never had. In a sense, they wouldn't be too far off.

"Dodger." Lampi waved the agent over. The bartender himself was the only respectable person in the room, and possibly the entire block. Despite the shabby nature of his bar, Lampi was always dressed to the nines and cleaning something. His hands in this case were occupying a wine glass, polishing it enough to where one could see most of the room in its reflection. The bar was mostly dirty, but there was a thick line where the daily grime ended and his working area began. "Who's the kid?" The bosnian asked.

"New blood for my group." Dodger said as he took a seat at the bar.

"You're twenty-one right?" Lampi asked as Oliver climbed onto the barstool. The kid froze up and stammered. The old bartender laughed and rolled his eyes. "Don't worry. I don't care so long as you have no intention of drinking."

The bosnian bartender knew Dodger was a mage and knew how he operated. He's the perfect example of the kinds of people an agent of Nightwatch should be acquainted with. He knew the inner goings of the city. He was physically imposing. He had an impeccable eye for detail, some deductive skills and knew when to keep his mouth shut.

"I don't care either sense none of the guys out here look tough." Dodger said.

"Not out here, but in the back." Lampi gestured to the door. The backroom was where any deals were made. There was also occasionally some gambling brokered by Lampi and people that he trusted.

"Sebastian's here tonight?"

"He and his whole gang." Lampi said with a nod. He leaned in to talk quietly. "This kid, he on the up and up?"

"He's trustworthy." Dodger answered. Even if Oliver had misgivings about being a mage in a secretive organization working from the shadows, Dodger believed he'd be the type to keep his mouth shut. Any worry of that nature Dodger could muster were unfounded though. Oliver had nothing but respect for the man who had saved him and opened up his eyes to the world of magic and monsters. Keeping Nightwatch's name out of Rachel's ears was proof enough of that.

"You looking for Crane, isn't something that's going to cause problems for me, is it?" Lampi was making more of a demand than he was asking a question. Sebastian Crane wasn't above exacting any vendetta he thought he could get away with. Everyone in that room, save for Oliver, was aware of that.

"Not even in the worst case scenario." Dodger said what he needed to ease the bosnian's mind.

"Well, good." Lampi said. "Because see that bloke there." He pointed to one of the drunkards. "He's one of Crane's new friends. And he buzzed the man when you were busy fraternizing with the patrons."

"Damn." Dodger whispered as he took a deep breath. He used his sensus to peer into the next room. There were five people: Sebastian Crane and his two lackies plus two others Dodger didn't recognize. He then got that tell-tale feeling of a burning gaze inside his head. The Hellfire Brats were keeping an ethereal eye on him. It was undoubtedly the work of

Marcus Kingfisher, the resident psychic of their little trio and one whose sensus rivaled that of Dodger's. The older agent motioned for his partner to follow his lead and the pair stepped into the next room.

Sebastian was completely relaxed. His little blonde girlfriend was running fingers through his shaggy black hair. His leather boots were propped onto the short table. He was presenting himself like a rockstar with his leather jacket fully open revealing the wife beater underneath. He was even doing a good job covering up that little burn mark on his neck that Dodger gave him once upon a time.

"Dodger." He smirked. His unnaturally violet eyes flashed for an instant as he sized Oliver up. "And a friend?" A smile crept on his face. That's when his two goons grabbed Dodger. To the right was Marcus Kingfisher, sporting a mohawk he dyed blonde for some gawdy reason. To the left was Michael Corvin. If not for his red eyes, he'd certainly pass for your typical street-tough.

Dodger rolled his eyes to let Oliver know to keep his mouth shut and that everything was going as the psychic had foreseen. Some other punk in a bandana patted him down before forcing him into a chair. As soon as Marcus and Michael took their hands off Dodger, he kicked his own feet up onto the table.

"Sabby sweetie, who is this?" The girl's voice was obnoxious, shrill, like a dog whistle. Sebastian had surely picked his girlfriend for a reason other than her voice. The woman was Jenny Eberle, a twenty-one year old addict who sold drugs and ripped off convenient stores when they weren't looking. A fitting partner for a lifelong trouble maker like Sebastian.

"Just an old friend, puddin." Sebastian said. "So, what do I owe this pleasure?"

"Felt it was time to check in." Dodger stretched nonchalantly. He was actually taking a quick eye of the surroundings. Red walls and a matching ceiling. With the bright torches lighting the room it really did look like

Hell. But thanks to Lampi's efforts alone there was also something cozy about it.

"Checking in? With a kid like that?" Sebastian mocked his counterpart.

"He's working the beat. This is his first time in a place like this so lay off." Dodger put his foot down and leaned forward. "His business here is my business, and I'm the one who has something to ask."

"Well, I'll give you an answer, if not a straight one." Sebastian was a crook, and a liar, but he was also smart. Not as smart as he thought he was but smart enough to know what Dodger was capable of.

"I heard Salma Robles had her house burned down." Dodger cut straight to the point.

"Did it now?" Sebastian nodded. "Shame, I haven't heard from her in a while."

"Not since she fired your ass?" Dodger prodded.

"Ha, I've been fired more times than a cannon and I never took retribution before. So, if you think I did it, you're mistaken."

"True you might not have burned down the houses of any former employer but you burned down plenty of other buildings. There's a first time for everything so forgive me if I refuse to think you're better than that."

"Why is an independent monster hunter and do-gooder so concerned about a single lady's house burning down?" Sebastian asked.

"It's not the only one." He said. "There's been a couple arsons–your specialty as I recall. Higher profile than the usual fare. I want to know if you've heard anything."

"If I had you're the last person I'd talk to."

"That's a lie, you'd tell me before Eliza Alcius. So, I'm not the last." It was a light joke but no less effective at cutting through any crap he may have been formulating.

"So, do you really think I had something to do with the arsons?" He clicked his jaw. His poker face was impeccable. He didn't get defensive. He didn't try laughing it off as an absurd possibility. He just sat there knowing exactly what led Dodger to that assumption.

"You're my prime suspect." Dodger admitted.

"If that were the case, I'd be a little more careful coming here. You can get hurt." That was true enough for most thugs. Most criminals would want to make their problems go away as fast as possible. If Sebastian was guilty, and believed Dodger was a threat, he'd do his best to make him go away. On the other hand, he knew Dodger wasn't someone who could be dealt with discreetly.

"I don't think you have what it takes to hurt me." Dodger called his bluff, knowing it was a dangerous game. Fighting any one of The Hellfire Brats would be hard for the Nightwatch agent. Fighting all three of them and protecting Oliver was out of the question. He needed to goad him into acting and making a mistake. He'd never risk a full blown immolation of Dodger in this situation. But if the agent could get under his skin he could urge him to act out just a bit, just enough to get something of use while he focused on punishment.

"You think you're top shit?" Sebastian laughed. "You're just a vigilante gang banger. And a traitor to your race." Bringing up that language was a sensitive subject for Dodger. With age came experience. Dodger was naturally a more gifted intellect than Sebastian or any of his goons. Sebastian made up the difference in talent with age and experience. He was five years Dodger's senior and therefore had five extra years of getting under people's skin. Dodger knew that when he entered this verbal duel and was going to use that to his advantage.

"And you think you're some sort of crime lord." Dodger let the weight of his words hit like a brick to the face. "But you're a punk-ass delinquent whose daddy left you when you were a kid. All this! The lights and the shady club and the goon platoon over there. It's all an act to cover up your daddy issues and inferiority complex. One of these days, the Order is going to catch up to you and I'm not going to be there to pull your sorry mug out of the fire you started."

It was only a matter of time before one of them goaded the other into making the first move. Sebastian had a numbers advantage if it turned into a brawl but for this bout those numbers proved a disadvantage. Jenny Eberle took offense to Dodger's comment. His sensus kicked in so he could see her actions a split second before she did them. He saw her pull the knife from her coat. He saw the trajectory of the blade. She was aiming not to cut him but merely to threaten him. That put him at an inherent advantage. With a snap of his hand he caught the blade between his fingers. Her grip was loose and the knife was ripped from her hand. Dodger caught the handle and aimed for Sebastian's hand. He saw it coming too, and got out of the way as the blade penetrated the wood of the table.

"Woah!" Oliver snapped back. For him everything looked like a blur.

"Bastard." Jenny hissed.

"Calm down Jenny." Sebastian said.

"You should keep your girl under control." Dodger smirked. Sebastian Crane was but one man after all. He could keep his cool. He could be as cool as an Antarctic June if need be. But the fools that followed him didn't have nearly the same amount of self-control that he did. Her reaction all but confirmed that they were involved, or knew who was. And he knew it. He'd be giving her a firm scolding after they were done here.

"Piss off and die." She cursed back at him.

"Pretty face, obnoxious voice, and an empty head. The two of you are perfect for each other." Dodger stood up and brushed off his jacket. "I'll keep my eye on you." He tried one last time to peer into Jenny's head for more information. Even though his sensus was far more attuned than any of theirs, it wasn't enough to get through any of the psychic barriers without Marcus blocking him out.

"What else is new?" Sebastian asked.

Dodger turned towards the door and Michael Corvin stopped him with a hand on his chest. Michael was the brawler of the group and preferred to talk with his fists. He was also the most protective of Sebastian and had been since they were kids. Dodger thought that if any of them would take a swing at him after mocking Sebastian it would be Michael. That's what he wanted.

The whole time Dodger was there, he was looking for something that could prove useful. He didn't need a level three sensus to know Michael would be easy to goad. Sebastian kept a tight lip so suspected he wasn't going to get information directly out of him. Worst case scenario, now he knew Dodger was coming for the arsonist. The added pressure could lead to a mistake on his part that'll lead back to him. Best case scenario, Dodger finds something more concrete. Jenny's reaction wasn't enough. She was too green. But Michael had a temper, was defensive of Sebastian, and would be much more likely to have something.

"Daddy issues?" Sebastian laughed. "Who needs a bastard like that when I've got a real family like this? The family you could have been a part of if you stopped being such a stubborn asshole."

"Better a stubborn asshole than a crooked prick." Dodger shot back. Michael tightened his grip and Dodger returned the favor by grabbing his collar. "You really want to do this, Corvin?"

"I owe you a good slug from last time." Michael growled.

"You get no protest from me but he'll probably hit you back." Sebastian noted. Michael didn't care. He surrounded his right fist in red flame. Dodger already had his corporis up to defend against the fiery punch. Even so, Michael was a big guy and the blow nearly knocked him down to the ground.

But that's when he got that special something he'd been looking for. Something didn't smell right. He had a scent, like that of a monster, or a demoran fresh out the gates. The Hellfire Brats were usually good about avoiding such smells. Whatever it was, was on Michael.

Dodger stood up and shoved him out of the way. He caught the source of the scent with his sensus, and flicked his fingers to pull it out of Michael's jacket and into his own all without anyone else noticing. He then turned the other cheek and motioned for Oliver to follow. There was no need to fight their way out now that they had what they came for.

Dodger checked his pocket as soon as he was back in the car. The object was an envelope wrapped with an embroidered ribbon. The embroidering and the seal were identical but foreign to the teen's eyes. He would have to take pictures and send it to Sir Nightwatch for more information.

"So…" Oliver broke the silence. "What was all that about you being a race traitor?" With a heavy heart Dodger sighed. He wouldn't answer immediately. He had spent too long keeping up appearances. It was common for people in his position to present themselves in a way that didn't attract the kind of attention they didn't want. To that end, Dodger drove his protege to an empty parking lot before telling him one of his many secrets.

"I was hoping you'd find out under more epic circumstances." Dodger admitted as he leapt from the car. With a snap of his fingers the illusion he–and many others–learned from a young age vanished in a sulfuric haze. He grew a few inches taller. Small goat horns sprouted from his head. The most drastic change came with his legs. They were the legs of a fawn, hooved and hairy. "I'm not from this world. I'm a Demoran, just like Sebastian Crane and the rest of The Hellfire Brats."

CHAPTER 12

The First Agent

If one would cross The Rift in the Middle East or much of Europe they would be greeted by a massive volcanic valley spewing sulfuric gasses in the air. In ancient times a few unlucky travelers found themselves in this valley and they equated it to the burning underworld that held the souls of the damned. In truth, if Hell did indeed exist it was not on the other side of The Rifts. Hell, Hades, Musphelheim, the humans had many names for that which laid across the veil but the demorans called it Sarph, which was their word for the most common gas in the atmosphere.

Sarph was just as ecologically rich as Earth. Its original sentient race went by many names but in the common tongues of man they were referred to as elves. In ancient times, various clans of elves sought strength through the beasts and monsters that ravished their lands. By combining their bodies with the appendages of these creatures, the demorans were born.

Since its origins The Celestial Order has treated all demorans as potential invaders. For many centuries they were imprisoned, tried and usually executed. As time went on, relations got better but were far from ideal. This was because much of Sarph was ruled by various tribes and empires. History and culture flowed in a very different direction than it did on Earth. Because of that, many demorans sought the stability of Earth over the tireless wars of the great demoran empires. The same could not be said in reverse. It was extremely rare for any human to make the journey across The Rift.

It was in mulling over these relationships that a certain mage first became aware of the stench of hypocrisy that had infected The Celestial Order. This culminated in a single event that would change the direction his life took. On October 28, 2002 he elected to save a young demoran child from certain death. That was the day this mage of considerable reputation cast away the light and glory to become Sir Nightwatch.

It was only a matter of time until this happened. Many close to this man had already glimpsed this inevitability. His devotion to his prior duties had grown as thin as his patience with those above him. It was not a peaceful divorce within the differing ideologies.

The Celestial Order was never right for Sir Nightwatch. He had a determination to destroy all evil and protect the innocent. He also had different ideas of what innocent and evil meant. The Celestial Order likes to treat all demorans as inherently evil. Even the good ones they tolerate, are discriminated against. Sir Nightwatch saw evil as a corruption. Evil–in his mind–is a choice. That choice is something someone so young would be incapable of making.

"Choosing to kill a child makes you evil." That was Sir Nightwatch's reasoning for killing a member of The Celestial Order. That murder put him at odds with the larger group. Charles Pickens pitied him and this child, and was the next to join him on this venture. Eventually the higher ups of The Celestial Order were forced to tolerate him. Now very few people knew about Sir Nightwatch and even fewer knew what exactly had happened between him and The Celestial Order.

On the very first day of 2003 Sir Nightwatch received one last message. It was from Grand Priest Gregory Pendragon himself. Gregory Pendragon was one whose history with Sir Nightwatch could only be accurately accounted in a volume all its own. All that mattered in this message though was that he was the one Sir Nightwatch respected and feared the most.

"You may continue doing what you feel is right. I know you are not a threat to anyone we would wish to protect. But know this, I will be watching. You will receive no help from The Celestial Order. Your name and accomplishments will be redacted from the records. You are on your own." That was the last time Sir Nightwatch had any communication with the man who had once mentored him. Thus he was left alone with Charles Pickens and a young demoran child.

That child's name was Donald Rogers. Charles personally oversaw his training. Like Sir Nightwatch, he had an unusual talent for magic. Typically, potential is inherited. Master Rogers was born to demoran parents who had no talent for magic. Perhaps that's why all these years later Sir Nightwatch held him in high esteem. To come from greatness and achieve greatness was a good thing. To come from nothing and achieve greatness was something to behold.

In 2014, Sir Nightwatch set Donald Rodgers up with a house in Shadowbrooke, outside St. Louis. Donald Rodgers quickly took to the nickname Dodger. Nobody but Sir Nightwatch himself knew why he had chosen Shadowbrooke to be Dodger's place of residence but the more informed could venture a few guesses. It had a long history of being a birthing ground of monsters. It could also be yet another phase in what he had started in 2012. Charles theorized that his main reasoning was to have his most trusted agent keep an eye on young Eliza Alcius, whose parents had a long and complicated history with Sir Nightwatch and who had been assigned as Arch Knight of St. Louis mere weeks before Dodger was sent to that area.

Whatever the case, Oliver Turner joining the ranks of Nightwatch had marked many changes. Bartleby had been the last of that collection of most heinous villains called The Gang of Eight. With his death many players had begun making moves to fill the gap in power. A storm was beginning to brew over St. Louis. It was a storm Sir Nightwatch was ready to fly headlong into.

CHAPTER 13

Eye of the Storm

O ctober was usually met with mild weather. It was in this month–
and its springtime counterpart–that the unpredictable Missouri
weather took a turn for the chaotic. There could be weeks where
it hit summer temperatures and wintry weather all in the span of a few
days. Unless one had familiarized themselves with the ebbs and flows of
midwestern weather one would not be able to understand the way its citizens took advantage of every nice day they had.

The true mark of time was the decorations. Throughout the entire
month of October every house in Shadowbrooke prepared for that night
when The Rift was at its widest. The night of ghosts and ghouls and candied
flavored spirits was on the horizon. For young Oliver Turner, it all looked
quaint compared to the vampyr he had seen.

Oliver never looked at Halloween as a time for fear. It was the time
of conquering fears. What better time to diminish one's fears of witches
and monsters than the holiday that made a mockery of their appearance in
order to get sugary sweets. Oliver was feeling much braver than in any year
before. His brush with death had made him stronger. He was still entirely
reliant on Dodger and the other mages that had gathered in Shadowbrooke
but while that made him self-conscious he rested easy knowing he was in
capable hands.

He mulled over what he knew and thought about everyone he had
met. He compared that to the simpler country life he had lived before

arriving here. He took pity on Dodger who had lost his parents at such an early age. He even pitied Eliza whose parents were alive but separated with one living in New York and the other living in Denmark. He took pity on Rachel who had lost her mom.

He wondered if Rachel knew that they shared that in common before they met. It made sense if his mother worked in Shadowbrooke as a mage for all those years. Perhaps she knew Rachel and her family. Getting personal information out of Rachel was proving a difficult task. She was awfully tight lipped about that subject and that subject alone.

A secretive person seemed to be the most popular Halloween costume amongst Oliver's friends. None of them had told Oliver everything. None of them told him the whole truth. None of them told him exactly what they saw in him. They just told him to get stronger, keep his grades up, and make associates.

Dodger was once again busy doing legwork for the case they had been investigating. The envelope he secured from The Hellfire Brats had a couple names, dates and addresses. Most of them were out of state with only one of them being in St. Louis. That address had also recently caught fire. There didn't seem to be any connection as far as the police or other interested parties could find. None of the other buildings on the list had burned down and none of the dates lined up with the fires.

The emblem on the seal matched the insignia of a real estate company in Chicago. The trail was still warm but the two agents of Nightwatch could tread no further. Chicago was a seed bed of crime and a hub for The Celestial Order. It was in that windy city that Eliza's direct superior–Deacon Sarah Mills–was stationed along with an arch knight and eight basal knights. It would be nigh impossible to secure transport, do all the necessary investigation and escape without being apprehended by either the knights or the mob.

"And here I was thinking St. Louis was bad." Oliver said upon hearing this reasoning.

"St. Louis is the minor leagues." Dodger said with one of his usual baseball metaphors. "Chicago is the third biggest city in America. St. Louis is the sixtieth."

"So then what are we going to do?"

"Stay on our toes. There's people far better suited to getting information out of a place like Chicago than we are. Keep getting stronger. Eliza was right about one thing, as you are now, you're more of a liability than an asset."

Oliver was at a loss. He didn't even know the name of the company and so he couldn't do his own research. He wanted nothing more than to help in every way he could even as he felt the familiar pit in his stomach that heralded his illness returning. It was here while shut in looking at his neighbor's halloween decorations that his father reminded him of something important to consider.

"Most mages don't fight monsters as their nine-to-five." Billy Turner would say. Whenever he would tell his son a story of heroes he would always remind the boy that true heroes lived lives outside of combat. Paladin Sir Henry Alcius was Eliza's father, as a paladin he held sway over all knights in the country and also ran a real estate company. The Grand Paladin Edgar Thatch was above him and commanded all the knights operating in North America and was a Senator from Vermont. Jobs like that, plus charitable donations and a tax exempt status was how The Celestial Order paid for food, housing and other supplies for their members.

The lengthy conversation about famous mages and their other jobs was interrupted by a knock on the door. It was none other than Rachel Rune coming to save Oliver from the stagnation of student life in order to take full advantage of the favorable fall weather. She was with Joey and Aayla and all of them were wearing silvery coats and scarves.

"We were going to hit the Loop and thought about inviting you." Rachel said. The Delmar Loop was a popular hangout spot in the city where highschoolers and college kids would indulge in all the trendy brands and food.

"I don't know, I'm kinda busy." Oliver tried getting out of it. As much as he liked hanging out with Rachel and her friends, deep down he knew it would only distract him. He had to be eager to make acquaintances, hesitant to make friends. At least that's the advice Dodger and Sir Nightwatch had given him.

"Oh come on, you have plenty of time to do whatever homework you got." Rachel beamed as she grabbed his hand.

"Yeah, that's part of the problem." Oliver half heartedly protested. Without making any pause Rachel's eyes narrowed and she pulled the boy in close. Her brown eyes borrowed deep into Oliver's soul. When she spoke this time it was nothing but a whisper.

"I want to know about you and Dodger?" The question caught him off guard. He had done well up to this point keeping anything magic related out of the time spent with the track star. With that said, he knew Dodger was friends with Rachel's sister–Brittany Rembrandt. And their father had known both of Oliver's parents a long time ago. In his desire to keep Nightwatch's secret, Oliver Turner had never attempted to figure out what all Rachel Rune knew.

"Just hanging out. We hit it off the first night we met and we've been up…playing baseball together at the park." The lie was thin and obvious and nobody in ear shot believed it.

"Uh-huh." She furrowed her brow again. "Look, I know it's none of my business but people our age shouldn't be running around town with people like Dodger. You just …you never know what's going to happen. I'd hate to see anyone getting hurt."

"You don't think I can defend myself?"

"I don't think it matters how much you can defend yourself. But no I don't." She slugged him in the arm as a joke. "You're still too short and scrawny." She laughed but Oliver wasn't able to play it off like she did.

"Yeah...I should really stay home." Oliver said. "I hope you have fun."

"You're really dead set on blowing me off aren't you?" Rachel said. "Very well, but you'll be missing out on some juicy information."

"Information?" Oliver asked.

"Oh so that did peak your interest." Rachel mused. "I'm not going to force anything. It's up to you whether you think I have valuable information."

Oliver relented and set aside his school work for the day. He was a native Missourian and it would be best to take advantage of this day regardless of what Rachel may or may not say. She had that effect on people. Soon Oliver would regret this decision and be eternally grateful that he followed Rachel into this adventure. Many pieces were moving simultaneously. The eye of the storm was closing. When it did Oliver would find himself facing his greatest challenge yet.

CHAPTER 14

Eliza Visits the Police Station

P art of the duties of all those at the rank of arch knight was working with all police precincts within their assigned area. Each arch knight is assigned one police liaison to act as a mediator between The Celestial Order and the various police departments they'll be working with. Special Agent Clint Finch had been police liaison in St. Louis for fifteen years. In that time he had worked with three different arch knights. The first was Harrison McCree and the second was Jeremy Dogget. Both of whom died in the line of duty. The third was Eliza Alcius.

Clint Finch had been contacted by Shadowbrooke PD in response to a mysterious phone call that Captain Johnathan Claymore received. Usually it was protocol for him to make contact with the arch knight himself but that was unnecessary. Whoever had called had instructed the police to contact Eliza themselves.

He had still managed to beat his partner to the precinct and talked with Commissioner Wilson. Commissioner Wilson didn't know any details as to the nature of this phone call. Captain Johnathan Claymore had been instructed by the caller not to say anything else until Eliza Alcius arrived.

Both veteran officers towered over the girl. Clint Finch was a man of broad shoulders and dusty brown hair. The man was old enough to be Eliza's father yet was far lower in rank as far as The Celestial Order was concerned. He was there for her benefit, nothing more. Commissioner Wilson had been dodging gunfire and writing traffic tickets for nearly thirty years.

The dark-skinned man was now bald and tired but no less dedicated to the particulars of his job. Even if he was willing to bend the rules if he thought it would benefit those he led.

Captain Johnathan Claymore was younger and more inexperienced but had an intimate knowledge of how the people of Shadowbrooke lived. His parents had been in and out of jail throughout most of his life. He had been raised on that side of the law and still became a police officer because he believed that better officers who better knew what life was really like would be better suited to fighting crime at its roots.

"Mind telling her what this is about Mr. Claymore." Commissioner Wilson's command was paired with a yawn.

"Yes of course." He pulled a file off the nearby chair and handed it to Eliza. She looked over the file which contained information about the recent arsons.. "We got a tip that these three incidents might be connected somehow. I can't shake the feeling that someone is suppressing the information we can use to link it up."

"That sounds like a job for the FBI or Internal Affairs." Eliza stated as she handed the file back to him. "I'm a celestial knight. Unless these arsons were perpetrated by a rogue mage then I have no obligation to assist you."

"That's the thing, there's just blanks where the cause of the fire should be." Jonathan Claymore said. "It's redacted. That could only mean one thing."

"They were obviously done by a mage and they don't want The Celestial Order involved." Eliza sighed. There were so many ways to start a fire, even without magic, that suppressing the cause of a flame was more suspicious than the flame itself. Whoever had caused this was so cautious that he created new evidence where there wouldn't have been any to begin with.

It was common for criminals to act this way. Altering the physical and chemical properties of the world made even the weakest mages too powerful for the police to handle. By that same merit, a man using magic in close proximity to someone with a celestial compass was easy to track. Celestial compasses are standard issue equipment for all members of The Celestial Order. And as an organization that technically worked outside the bounds of local and federal law, this meant anyone wanting to get away with magic based crimes had to take extra precautions to keep The Celestial Order off their trail. It was more than worth the price of paying someone off.

"So will you look into it?" Captain Claymore asked.

"Yes, but I need to know who tipped you off." Eliza was assuming that whoever made the phone call was someone close to the case and may be targeted by the criminals if they discovered he had talked.

"It was definitely a man but he never gave his name." Captain Claymore said. "He just said the dates and the police code for arson, then said that The Celestial Order needs involvement."

"And he contacted you?" Clint Finch asked.

"I just happened to answer the phone." Captain Claymore shrugged.

"Curious." Eliza raised a knuckle to her lip, a normal gesture for when she was thinking. The first names that popped in her head were Dodger and Oliver. Dodger was the only one who had stuck his nose in such business in the past but getting her involved this way wasn't something he would do. Perhaps Oliver did this without his approval. If it was one of them, how did they find the connection?

"Any other thoughts, Arch Knight Alcius?" Commissioner Wilson asked.

"Not at the moment. I will report these findings to my superiors. Proceed with caution and report any arsons directly to either Special Agent Finch or myself."

"Yes ma'am." Captain Claymore nodded.

Shortly after she left she was informed about a fourth incident. It had happened just one night earlier and so hadn't been officially reported yet.

The home of Garret Bledsloe–a radio technician for a local TV station who lived in South St. Louis had caught fire. The connection wasn't immediately clear but the company that had insured the place was the same as a few of the others. Overall finding a unifying factor was futile. There was none for there was no singular motive connecting all these arsons. There was only a chain of overlapping circumstances and information that connected the arsons like a chain wrapped around the entire St. Louis metropolitan area.

One of the dates jumped out at the young arch knight. It was the same date as the vampyr attack and the address was close enough to her home where she would have been able to sense the crime and intervene if she wasn't elsewhere. That was also a very common trope for those criminals that wished to avoid conflict with The Celestial Order.

She went back home and typed up reports for her superiors to read through. Eliza was a girl of many unconscious habits. Writing reports, knowing her father could read them if he so desired, brought out the worst of these habits. She would bite and pick at her nails to the point of drawing blood. Her fingers and lips would become calloused from picking at any dead skin she noticed. There was only one person she wasn't ashamed to show this side of herself to. That was her partner and childhood friend Amelia Petrochilos.

"You're playing with your bottom lip." Amelia said. She moved behind Eliza's chair and put warm hands on her boss' shoulders. Eliza was so much more confident when playing music, reading books or battling monsters. Dealing with the higher ranks of The Celestial Order never came as easily. Amelia hadn't the authority nor the disposition to ever challenge her and so her presence was often soothing for the arch knight in these times. "What did you notice?"

"Between these targets, the various police stations involved, the recent vampyr battle and our mysterious informant, I think the scope could be larger than we realize." Eliza said.

"Thinking there's others that haven't been reported?"

"It's a possibility. Without access to our extensive records I'm not going to find anything deeper than what these files say at face value."

"I'll get coffee started."

"That would be nice. I think I'm going to sit on these for a while though."

"That's not like you?" Amelia said. "Do we have a big test coming up in school or something?"

"No...well yes we actually do but that's not it." Eliza bit her thumb and chose her next thought carefully. "Only one person was hurt. Salma Robles ran into the fire after it had already started. Even if these are magic related arsons, I'm out of my purview if nobody gets hurt. I'm supposed to protect people, not hunt down criminals like an attack dog. Who is the informant? And why does he want me involved?"

Eliza's attention was stolen by a familiar presence turning onto her street. She cursed under her breath as she put the file away to greet her unwanted visitor. She quickly swung the door open before Dodger's loathsome self had the chance to knock.

"I don't recall inviting you." Eliza snipped.

"Oh well excuse me for a cordial visit." Dodger said. "I happened to be in the neighborhood looking to stick my nose in something exciting and I thought you might have some work that was dropped on your lap that you'd see as beneath you."

The convenient timing of Dodger's visit had not gone unnoticed. Eliza tended to suspect him of all sorts of trouble. He had been nothing but a headache for her for all these years. The timing hadn't been an accident. He did know about the file and was wishing to get a peek. He knew it was a long shot but he could also tell from Eliza's nails that whatever she was working on had frustrated her.

"None of your damn business." Eliza hissed.

"Well, I know you're busy. If it's something small I can take it off your hands."

Eliza's response was to shove him away from the door and slam it. That was the response he was expecting and it all but confirmed that she was working a case that was juicy enough for her to want to do things herself. It was evidence that she did receive some information that Dodger wished to see and he was completely sure it was about the same case he had been working on. After all, Captain Johnathan Claymore wasn't the only one that had been contacted by that man of mystery.

CHAPTER 15

The Immolation of Oliver Turner

Usually by this time of the year Oliver would have a perpetually runny nose and headache. By the end of the month he would start getting flu symptoms and be bedridden for a week. When he was little he would get sick all the time but ever since hitting puberty that sickness was only seasonal. This time though his symptoms had yet to start. He thanked the stronger body he had been developing. Rachel gave herself some credit for that fact.

When they had first met Oliver claimed to like video games. While he still did partake in that hobby in his free time he had not done so with Rachel. This was the first suspicious thing the teen athlete had noticed. She kept her introductions blunt in order to gauge people's gut reactions. Those gut reactions tended to be more honest than the carefully articulated ones. So when Rachel invited Oliver to play video games and he turned her down, it was strange. Strange still he always joined her for jogs and asked to hang out whenever physical activity was involved.

At first Rachel thought he might just have a thing for her, or a thing for cute girls in jogging clothes. That didn't seem to be the truth though. If he was physically attracted to her he did a good job hiding his intentions. Then there was the matter with Dodger. Knowing that they spent time together gave Rachel a clue. It was one she ignored and wished would not lead to where it usually does. This was nothing more than wishful thinking.

"We're almost there." Rachel huffed as she spun around. They had spent all day at Delmar before parting ways with Aayla and Joey. She then asked him to jog with her to the nearest park.

"I need a break." Oliver was relieved when they arrived at the park and he slumped his way to the nearest bench for a rest. He envied Rachel's boundless energy and the physique that came with her lifelong interest in athletics. The pair of motherless teens sat on the bench together waiting to see which one would broach the subject first.

"I've actually been meaning to ask you, what's your relationship with Dodger all about?" Rachel was the one who broke the subject. Oliver had been dreading this line of question for obvious reasons but he also respected and trusted Rachel.

"We just hang out." He attempted to avoid further inquiry but he wasn't going to get out that easily.

"Ah yeah, I get bros before hoes but it just seems different with you two." Rachel was leaning onto her own pool of information. Oliver after all was still new to Shadowbrooke, new to the life of mages, he had yet to learn much about the people he saw every day.

"It's nothing really." Oliver insisted.

"Well, if he's just a bro then think of me as a bro." She leaned closer.

Oliver's heart started racing. He always thought Rachel was cute but this was the first time she made his heart race like this. Her alluring physique forced him to place his mental defenses elsewhere.

"What's so special about him anyway?" Her stare bore through his own. The question kept ringing in his ears. Her eyes darted back and forth as if she were reading his thoughts.

"It's not like that I swear!" The thought that crossed Oliver's mind was enough to throw his mind off her proximity. It was also enough to derail Rachel's own train of thought since it was nowhere near what she was implying. "I am absolutely not gay."

There was a pause followed by laughter. Oliver was too innocent for his own good. Rachel was no fool. She wasn't the innocent flower child her father thought she was. She had lived in Shadowbrooke all her life and as such had indulged in things a woman her age shouldn't. If she thought Oliver had a crush on anybody she would have come right out and said it. She knew better than to bottle up emotions like that.

"To hell with it." She said as her laughter stopped. "I didn't ask directly because I refuse to get involved but...I know about Dodger."

"Know what?" Oliver's eyes widened. In the back of his mind he should have suspected that Rachel knew all along. He didn't trust her enough. He didn't trust her with his own thoughts and now she was echoing information he had only recently been privy to.

"That he's a demon." She whispered. "And that he hunts monsters and competes with that Eliza girl."

"What? You're talking crazy." Oliver lied instinctively. Truth was if someone had told him that just a few weeks earlier he would have assumed they were crazy. Oliver had nobody to blame but himself for not confirming with Dodger who knew what about his dealings.

"I'm not stupid Oliver. I can see it. You've gone through some mage training." She clenched her fists on her legs. "I know what kind of danger you've been putting yourself in. It's the only thing that makes sense."

"So, you do know that much?" Oliver sighed.

"I've always known. My Sister is ...well she and Dodger go way back. She stopped getting involved with that part of his life about two years ago. One too many close calls."

"And you?"

"I'm a pacifist. I don't want to hurt anybody or anything. I want to be a doctor." Rachel giggled.

"So then why tell me what you know?"

"Because I don't want any more of my friends getting hurt." She said. "Stuff like that should be left to the people who know what they're doing. It's dangerous."

"Everything is dangerous at first. That's why you train."

"Oliver, I won't force you or give you an ultimatum. I just want you to know, I don't approve, and you don't have to lie to me."

"I ...won't." The statement itself was a lie. Oliver didn't want to worry her so, as far as she had to know he was still training. But with that, a thought crossed his mind. Did Rachel know about Nightwatch? It seemed unlikely but Oliver should assume nothing after a conversation like this.

Rachel took a sip of water and then lamented its empty contents. She spotted a vending machine and jogged off to replace her beverage. As soon as she was out of ear shot a hot wind blew onto Oliver's back. A shadow of a man with a mohawk loomed over Oliver. A hand slammed against his mouth as the figure leaned in close to his ear.

"I thought she'd never leave." The voice sent a shiver down Oliver's spine. Someone was leaning against the bench. "Oliver, right?"

Oliver recognized this man as Marcus Kingfisher of The Hellfire Brats. He wore clothes one would expect from a man enjoying the summer, not someone at a park in autumn. Blue flames manifested in his free hand to intimidate Oliver into staying silent. The boy then felt himself ripped from the bench and careening skyward. His screams were muffled by the hand of Marcus as the demoran revealed his true form. His legs became that of an eagle. His entire upper body flickered in blue flames forming the visage of a phoenix. Multiple hands of telekinesis kept Oliver from moving around too much as he was held high above the ground. Rachel and the other park goers were less than ants from this view. Meanwhile Marcus struck an imposing immolating figure.

"Your buddy Dodger took something from us and now were going to make you pay." Marcus said. He clutched Oliver in his talons and flew away. The agent of Nightwatch had been kidnapped by The Hellfire Brats.

CHAPTER 16

The Shark of Chicago

They say only cowards lurk in the shadows. If one were to ask Francis Puffin he would say only a fool conducts his business in broad daylight. Discretion, control, caution, this is what separates the higher class of criminals from the punks that get caught by the cops on a weekly basis. And when one deals with mages, it's not just the feds and the coppers they have to worry about.

Francis Puffin had been running the streets of Chicago for as long as he could remember. The child of Hungarian immigrants had been born into it. His father was a young man when prohibition ended in the 1930s. He was a child when the crime families started turning their focus to other illegal avenues of finance. Francis Puffin lasted this long because he was always careful about who to trust, who to pay off, who to blackmail, and who to order around to do his bidding. It was because of this ruthlessness tempered by age that he was nicknamed The Shark of Chicago. Most people wouldn't expect a pudgy old shark like him to call the shots of one of the biggest gangs in the city and yet here he was.

By those merits he was getting nervous about the dealings in St. Louis. Monopolization of property and politics disguised as insurance scams disguised as arsons. There were a lot of fingers in the pot. Too many for his liking. With a dozen or so people in the know, one of them was certainly a snitch.

"It'll be fine." Damien Crow assured. Thus a glimpse into the true mind behind this plot had elected to visit the old mobster. He specialized in subterfuge and extortion. The rule of thumb here in Chicago was that "Blackfire" always chose the winning side. Elections, criminal trials, even events on the national scale swayed to his tongue. He and Francis Puffin never argued about who was in whose pocket. They were long time partners in all the things that wouldn't make the evening news.

"But if one of those kids cracks?" Francis Puffin tried arguing against the use of a small-time gang like The Hellfire Brats. They had no fear of the mob, no loyalty to Damien Crow and nothing to lose by screwing them over.

"Then they will be throwing themselves under the bus. They know nothing of you. They think that you and your real estate business are the victims. They think you're the one coming after them. They will be the perfect fall guys, and when they do fall they will not fall quietly. Anti-demoran sentiments are still high in St. Louis after the mess Chris Crimson left five years ago. They will find it hard to believe that a demon mage as talented as Sebastian Crane could take orders from anybody. Especially a citizen of your standing."

"If you say so." Francis Puffin took a puff from a cigar as he dealt some cards. He preferred not talking business in front of the help, but Damien Crow was a hard man to reach. He preferred talking business in person. The only other people with them were Jack Ogle–bodyguard and handyman of Francis Puffin–and an old associate from Boston named Allistor Briggs.

Damien Crow was a tall man with broad shoulders and inky black hair that was combed backwards with gel. He was conventionally handsome with chiseled facial features and a commanding voice. Jack Ogle was a tall thin man with shoulder length brown hair and a goatee. He didn't look like much but he was quite a marksman and had some skill as a mage. Mr. Briggs was shorter than the other two, but still taller than Francis

Puffin. Small wire-framed glasses sat on his hawkish nose. His brown-ish-blonde hair was styled with the bangs standing up straight. He was the one who introduced the mobster to the journalist and served as the pipeline between Chicago and New York's crime lords.

"Say boss, did you hear what happened to Sharsky?" Jack Ogle asked as he looked at his cards.

"I heard he got grabbed by the feds." Francis Puffin answered. Sharsky was an associate of theirs who had been nabbed three nights earlier. He was also in charge of handling the vampyrs the cabal was using in their current schemes. Not much was known about his apprehension and so the mobster had to cut his losses for now.

"That's the craziest thing." Jack Ogle said. "My buddy Vinny was scouting out a place near the park when it happened. He says it wasn't the feds. It was a mage. A powerful one at that."

"Likely just an overzealous knight." Damien Crow assured.

"None of the knights round there use shadows." Jack Ogle argued. "This guy strung up Sharsky with shadows. By the time the knights got there he was already a goner."

"Strung up with shadows? Preposterous." Damien Crow folded his hand. "Shadows have no mass, no physical properties. Even with magic you can't manipulate shadows. Whoever this was merely used something meant to look like shadows."

"How he fights doesn't matter." Francis Puffin interjected. "If he put the squeeze on Sharsky, he could be coming for any one of us next. Could be one of them celestial crusaders that roam the countryside. Could be a knight from out of town. Could be a rival gang just got themselves a heavy hitter."

"Or it could be that Nightwatch fella." Allistor Briggs said as he raised the bet. As a man from the east coast he was perhaps the only person in Chicago that night who had ever heard that name.

"Nightwatch?" Francis Puffin asked.

"Back east, about three years ago now." Mr. Briggs spun his tale. "I was runnin' guns with ole Zolomon McKay up in New York. The knights came bursting through his door and he ran. He called to meet me up in Central Park so we could make a break for it. By the time I got there, he was dead on a lamp post. I kept a low profile but I heard Sir Henry Alcius himself say that it was the work of a man named Nightwatch."

"Are you sure about this?" The old mobster inquired.

"He's just an urban legend around the East Coast." Damien Crow said. He had heard from some of his fellow elite journalists that there were rumors about a certain mage hiding in the shadow of The Celestial Order. "He's a piece of disinformation The Celestial Order started spewing to scare any criminals wise to their methods. The Celestial Order has rules of engagement. Nightwatch allegedly has no such rules. He's a scare tactic since The Celestial Order are far too few in number to properly police the world."

"I heard he was one of them." Allistor Briggs said. "When Chris Crimson was still around I heard that someone had battled the Grand Inquisitor and won. It was around this time that rumors started spreading about a man who fights with shadows."

"Therein lies the sad lie of his existence." Damien Crow said. "Nobody has beaten the current Grand Inquisitor. Not many people in this world could even put up a fight."

"You seem pretty shaken at his name." Francis Puffin noted. If someone was part of The Celestial Order and wished to leave, besting a warrior as capable as the Grand Inquisitor was a great way to show that you weren't worth the trouble of hunting. "How can someone who peddles in propaganda be so sure that he is not reciting propaganda himself?"

"As someone who has weaved his fair share of fairy tales I know the danger of such falsehoods." Damien Crow explained. "Whether you and I acknowledge his existence doesn't matter. If those below us fear him, they'll get sloppy and will be easier to catch."

"Now you share my sentiments."

"I merely see where such cautions come from. That's why I only work with those who know how to do their jobs. It's why I do what I can to throw any would-be hero off our case. In fact, a little bird told me that someone has made a connection between the arsons. I already have someone preparing to make it look far more political than it actually is."

"You did this without notifying me?"

"Mr. Puffin, I thought you of all people would understand the subtleties of subterfuge. Have I ever led you astray?"

"No, I suppose not."

That was the last time anything remotely related to their business ventures was brought up. None of this information about mages in the shadows sat right with any of them. All four of these individuals found themselves on high alert as the night fell. Eventually the night of cards was over and Francis Puffin headed off to bed.

The conversation from earlier had spooked the old Hungarian enough to where his mind began playing tricks on him. He could have sworn the shadows in his room were moving for but fleeting seconds upon entering. His bedroom window was cracked open and so he assumed it was the typical Chicago wind rustling some of his curtains.

What Francis Puffin didn't know was that someone had been in his room. Gloved hands that were not his were the ones that cracked the window open. Someone had a network of informants that could rival any mobster. Upon putting the squeeze on Sharsky he was able to find a missing link in this ever complicated chain of events. Had Francis Puffin's room not been soundproof he may have even heard the cackle of Sir Nightwatch as he made his way to St. Louis.

CHAPTER 17

The Spark of Conspiracy

T he events of October 12, 2018 were national news. The story of a cop shooting an unarmed teen had already lit the spark that was sweeping across the entire nation before the body could even be declared dead. It was such a sensational tragedy that nobody had even thought to report the kidnapping that had transpired mere moments later.

Shadowbrooke PD were under fire even though nobody knew any of the particulars in this case. Damien Crow only made the fires worse, using this death and the arson of Donovan Brown's home just a month earlier to prosthelytize about hatred and violence in this country. This was a tragedy. As the facts came in nobody would deny that. It was a tragedy for both sides, the particulars of which nobody would know until the year was long over. The youth had been a criminal delinquent but he was running after seeing a vampyr. The officer had responded to a call about an attempted arson. The young demoran matched the description he had been given. He reached for his gun and the youth retaliated in fear, tackling the officer. The officer in question had no control of his body when his gun was drawn and discharged. None of the witnesses could see the man in a black stealth suit orchestrating the entire crime.

The only person that believed something more foul was afoot was Captain Johnathan Claymore. He knew the story of mages all too well. He knew well enough that anything was possible when mages were involved and that it was best to treat things with skepticism. The masses on the other hand would ignore that possibility until given a motive. The fact the officer was responding to a potential arson struck Captain Claymore as odd enough to look into any connection between this shooting and the arsons he had looked into.

He was not the only one who saw a potential connection. Mayoral candidate Donovan Brown must have sensed a greater purpose to the chaos that now enflamed the streets of Shadowbrooke. As soon as the news hit he had summoned Captain Claymore and Arch Knight Eliza Alcius to his campaign office to discuss something.

His campaign office was across the street from a park. While standing beside his desk, glass in hand, he could watch children play on the swings and merry-go-round. It was for those children that he had gotten into politics in the first place. He wished to better manage funds to give kids better opportunities. If he could keep more kids off the streets, if he could give them healthy alternatives to joining gangs, it would have all been worth it.

That's why even though he was not above the corrupting power of politics, he was always on the straight and narrow when it came to legal matters. He was still young and idealistic for a politician and so that corrupting influence had yet to take hold.

"I'm glad the both of you made it." He turned to greet his guests.

"If you don't mind me asking, why is Captain Claymore here?" Eliza Alcius asked. There was no malice in her tone. She had already suspected the reason. It was, however, uncouth for her to be called alongside an officer without her police liaison.

"Trustful people are a rare commodity." He explained as he sat at his desk. "Power is a corrupting force. I wanted someone who knew the gist of the situation but was enough of an unknown entity in order to be away from the prying eyes of the corrupt."

"I'm not sure I understand your meaning." Captain Claymore said.

"You're too low on the ladder to be seen as a threat." Eliza's comment struck a blow to the officer's pride. Even at the rank of Captain, nobody knew who he was. Those who looked into things saw little more than a perfect record. Every arrest was by the books. There were no allegations of brutality or harassment. His gun had seldom even left its holster and had never once been fired.

"And you, Eliza Alcius, have quite a history of speaking out against corruption." On his desk the politician had an open file detailing everything there was to know about the both of them. Before running for election, he had been a county clerk and had made enough connections there to get any file on anyone he had desired. "Both of your parents are from esteemed lineages. You were knighted at the age of twelve. Not unheard of, but rare. Then, you were dumped in a minor city. Usually someone of your inheritance would have been named arch knight in a city like New York, Toronto, or Paris, not St. Louis. I wonder why."

Eliza Alcius was put off by that notion. It flashed upon her face for only a second before she regained her composure. Within The Celestial Order rank brought about prestige but more important was your assignment. She technically held the same power as every other arch knight in The Celestial Order. Yet when compared to the arch knights of the great cities of the world she would be belittled. The second daughter of Sir Henry Alcius and Dame Anne Rosen, left in a backwater city in a flyover state. If she was truly worthy of that name she would be in New York or London or Berlin. Even Copenhagen was more prestigious due to its historical connection to the founding of The Celestial Order. That is what many of her former classmates and peers had thought. The truth was however more nuanced.

"My father, Sir Henry Alcius–the Paladin of the United States of America, Sir Edgar Thatch–Grand Paladin of North America, and Gregory Pendragon–the esteemed Grand Priest of The Celestial Order, all pledged that if I can make a name for myself in a small city like this by my eighteenth birthday, then I will be promoted to Deacon and be next in line to be the Paladin of this country."

Even though she was allowed to make that claim at her own discretion she usually hid that agreement. It was the exact kind of backdoor deal and nepotism she had spoken out about while still attending the academy. She had argued with many of her teachers and superiors about the need for each individual to prove themselves because she always felt she had much to prove herself. She only told them because she felt that the politician looking for a promotion and the do-gooder officer would understand that feeling more than anyone in her family.

"Well, don't know how much of a name you can make here. But if you are, this is the time." Donovan Brown assured her.

"This is about those arsons?" She surmised.

"Precisely. And I think that young man who was shot is involved as well." Donovan Brown sighed and took a drink. "I was approached by a man named Briggs. I was promised an easy victory in the upcoming election if I turned a blind eye to the arsons. When I refused, my house was targeted."

"This Briggs, what did he look like?" Captain Claymore asked as he took out a notepad.

"I don't know, we only spoke on the phone. But ever since then, my life has been hell. I've been tanking in the polls. My reputation as a community leader has come under fire. And I've gotten numerous death threats."

"Comes with the territory of politics." Captain Claymore stated.

"I'm of the opinion that people should decide for themselves. Not be shrouded by the lies of crackpots like Damien Crow." Donovon Brown stood back up. "He was a good supporter right up until my house burned down. Now he rarely ever reports on anything about me except my failing poll numbers. Ms. Alcius, I think someone is trying to have me killed. And I want you two as my witness that someone from out of our jurisdiction is using a group of small-time criminals to get their way."

"Do you have any proof?" Captain Claymore asked.

"I was given this file." He tapped the folder on his desk. "I haven't read through all of it, but it involves one Francis Puffin, a well known entity up in Chicago. I have friends of my own that warned me about him."

"How did you get a hold of this?" Eliza Alcius asked as she picked up the folder.

That was enough talking as far as a certain observer was concerned. Unbeknownst to the three in that room a fourth person had become aware of the meeting and was being paid a handsome sum to make sure Donovan Brown stayed quiet. Not even Eliza Alcius could detect him through his stealth suit. She had no clue of his presence until he launched a green fireball from his perch at the park. There was no loud bang, only the *whoomph* of the entire building being lit ablaze.

Eliza to her credit acted quickly as soon as she sensed the attack. Using telekinesis she ripped Donovan Brown, desk and all, away from the window. The fireball hit the window as Captain Claymore and Donovan Brown slammed into the opposite wall. The arch knight had jumped over the flying desk and used her animus to form a barrier between the flames and the potential victims.

A second fireball hit the barrier and shattered it. Eliza commanded the sprinklers to burst into action. She commanded all the water to leave the pipes immediately and with a swirl of her hand she managed to stop the spreading fire. She then scouted the park for the assailant. Nothing stuck out but often in these situations the lack of something is evidence. She located the spot where the flows of mana stopped and aimed a focused blast of her animus directly at it.

The assailant managed to avoid the blast but the fall to the ground forced his stealth suit to malfunction. Suits like that only worked if the person wearing it wasn't in direct light and without the shade of the tree he could now only lightly camouflage himself. This was not enough to escape even the most untrained eyes.

"I'm pursuing the assassin. Get him to safety!" Eliza barked.

"Yes Ma'am." Captain Claymore gasped.

The assassin ran from the scene of the crime with Eliza Alcius hot on his trail. Meanwhile Johnathan Claymore grabbed the files on Donovan Brown's desk for safe keeping. If someone was willing to kill over this it must be important.

CHAPTER 18

Oliver is Captivity

While Sir Nightwatch made his way through Chicago Oliver had been kidnapped. The next day he awoke to the sound of sirens. It was the same day that Eliza would encounter the mob's enforcer and police were too busy dealing with the chaos that reigned outside to begin the manhunt.

The abduction itself was the worst part. Sharp wind pierced through Oliver's sweatpants as he flew through the air. He flew faster than any roller coaster and had anything been stored in his bladder he would have embarrassed himself. The thought of fighting back in that situation was terrifying. That was why the first thing Marcus Kingfisher did was throw him into the air. An aerial battle was suicide for those who couldn't fly.

Oliver had paid attention to where they were going. From the abduction point they had headed east. It was one of the worst areas of St. Louis and one Oliver would be hesitant to wander around alone. At some point, Marcus threw him towards a building. Oliver's momentum slowed as the thug controlled his movements and the movement of the building's walls. The brickwork moved to open up by his command. Marcus followed him through the apartment's maw before resealing the brick wall.

"What do you want?" Oliver shouted.

"You and your friend stole from us. Nobody steals from us." Marcus said.

"What are you talking about?" Oliver played dumb. He knew what he was after but even if he had the envelope it was too late. The contents of that message had already been relaid to Sir Nightwatch. The damage from the theft was done and there was no going back.

"Just what do you plan to accomplish?" Marcus asked. His clawed foot pinned Oliver to the wall. "Are you working for somebody else? Is it The Celestial Order?"

"I just follow Dodger's lead." Oliver pleaded.

"Don't play dumb with me!" Marcus covered the palm of his hand with a chemical substance he had done some research on. He knew the nature of the compound enough to create it from any liquid. With that poison he struck Oliver across the face. "I just infected you with a toxin. It won't kill you, but it'll hurt like a bitch. Now, tell me where you get your information from."

"I already told you you're barking up the wrong tree!"

"Liar." He smacked the boy again. The vision in one of Oliver's eyes began to blur. His ears were ringing. His heart throbbed and burned. It felt like thousands of little needles were drilling into his face. "Look here you little twerp. The only reason you're still alive is because we want information out of you."

"Dodger's the only one that would know. And good luck making him talk."

Marcus gave up on this interrogation. He once again left Oliver alone, chained to the wall. He hadn't been able to eat anything. He was left with nothing but a bucket to use as his toilet. His face was swollen too much for him to get comfortable. He couldn't sleep to pass the time. All he could do was listen to the sirens and pray for rescue.

All those he hoped would find him had no chance of locating him. The Hellfire Brats had chosen this makeshift hideout well. They all lacked the means to track him down. Oliver couldn't even bargain for himself if he wanted to. He knew nothing of value to the thug. Even if he did want to spoil what he knew of Nightwatch they wouldn't believe him. All he could do was wait.

Or he could escape. He had no clue how he would go about doing that but Marcus had rightfully assumed Oliver had yet to succeed in even the simplest forms of magic. There was nothing special about the chains or the walls. If he could just project his will onto these chains perhaps he could free himself.

From the light coming in through the window Oliver was able to surmise that he had been in this room for nearly twenty-four hours. Marcus only interrupted him once an hour to give him something to drink and ask if he was ready to talk. Each time he would leave Oliver would fight through the hunger and pain to focus on the chains.

He knew how locks worked. He knew that the key would trip a set of pins thus allowing the lock to move. If he could just use telekinesis to trip the lock he could free himself. He closed his eyes and took deep breaths. He imagined what the inner workings of the lock must look like. He flexed the muscles of his hand as he imagined the pins of the lock moving. A faint yellow light illuminated the dimly lit room. He could feel power flowing through his body. Just as that power was reaching its climax it was cut off.

Oliver could only feel the boot against his face followed by the cold grimy bricks as his head was kicked into the wall. Marcus had sensed his attempt at escape. He was The Hellfire Brats' resident psychic and the only real hope for escape was to best him.

That was something Oliver couldn't do, and wouldn't be able to do for a long time. Even if he snapped the lock easily, Marcus would be there to knock him out and he'd be back at square one.

By the time Oliver awoke it was night time. He could no longer gauge how long he had been in confinement. His mind was divided between the wounds to his head and the hunger clawing at his stomach. He clung to what little hope he had. There were surely people looking to rescue him. So long as he clung to survival he would get out of this eventually. If Marcus desired to kill him he would have died at the park, not been taken as a captive.

Oliver had to keep trying. His next attempt would be his last. He would do the same thing without closing his eyes. If he could bait an attack from Marcus he could maybe counter and knock him out or take the key or find something that would help his position. He had felt a yellow glow the last time right before the thug intervened. If he could do that again maybe it would have a desirable effect.

Marcus sensed the buildup of mana before Oliver was even aware of what he was doing. He moved to kick Oliver in the ribs but before either of them could see what was going to happen, a pulse of yellow light blasted the thug into the opposite wall. Oliver was thrown backwards by the force of his own attack and fell against the wall. Marcus cursed under his breath as blue energy gathered at his fingertips.

At that moment they were no longer alone. At the same time Oliver had manifested his animus, a third figure had entered the room. A chilling laugh echoed off the walls. The whole room went dark, save for two burning amber eyes. Oliver's attempts to escape had not gone unnoticed by those outside. Had Oliver not seen this figure before he would have surely been more terrified than his captor.

Threads of darkness struck Marcus in the head. The demoran fell and rolled over back to his feet. The captor foresaw the finger on the trigger. He saw the path the bullets would take before the gloved hand could squeeze any tighter. The sound of gunfire heralded a trio of bullets each one passed through the burning form of Marcus. The gunman was impressed by the demoran's ability to change the form of his body fast enough to avoid the fatal shots. But it would take more than that to defeat this vortex of shadows.

Marcus summoned a torrent of blue flames to combat the shadows. The fire was blocked by thick shadowy maws and a spark of orange flames.

A strong leather boot kicked the demoran in the ribs and when he tried fighting back he was thrown into the wall and struck repeatedly by the mysterious dark specter.

Marcus molded his body into flames and made way to the window. He crashed through the glass and retreated. He had no idea what he was up against. He also did not know how lucky he was that this dark specter of justice had elected to spare him for now. The shadows shrunk back into the cloak of this shrouded savior.

"Mr. Turner." The cold assuring voice of Sir Nightwatch reached the ears of his agent.

"Sir…Nightwatch?" Oliver coughed out. "You found me."

"It was thanks to your own attempts at escape that I was able to track you here. Now, are you hurt?"

"My face…poison." He knelt down and grabbed the boy's face. With a knife in hand he made a small incision to let the toxin out. It was a complicated procedure that required him to use his sensus to locate the particles of the toxin, command them to leave through the small wound, and do so without further damaging Oliver's face. It was a favored technique used by many medical specialists within The Celestial Order but Sir Nightwatch had learned it from a heinous fiend who used it for torture.

The blue toxin gathered into the air and then coated the blade. The blade took on a bluish hue as runes materialized along its cutting edge. Within seconds, Sir Nightwatch had turned an ordinary dagger into an enchanted one, albeit one only temporarily so. Sir Nightwatch was a man of many talents but binding one's soul to a weapon to permanently enchant it was a skill known only by the most practiced of craftsmen.

"So that you may grow stronger from this ordeal." He whispered.

"I'm sorry. I couldn't stop him."

"Don't mind that, Mr. Turner. The opportunity will come again." He stood back up and hoisted Oliver onto his feet.

"You let him get away?" Oliver said.

"If I defeated him now, what use would that be?" He chuckled. "I came to St. Louis, on the heels of a threat more troubling than The Hellfire Brats themselves. I feared the mages here would not be enough. But now, we are in the final stages. By the end of this year, The Hellfire brats will be smothered, Crow's wings will be clipped, and all of those connected will be facing justice."

CHAPTER 19

Eliza Gives Chase

Eliza was far from perfect. Perfection was impossible. She knew her own shortcomings well enough. Her sensus in particular was less refined than many of her peers. It had been the last of the tria-ethos she had obtained. She was a caster through and through. Her biggest strength was her animus and the rest of her body was only good enough to keep her own mana from overwhelming her.

So she had only detected the assailant when he had already launched his attack. Dodger and Amelia would have been able to see it coming far sooner. What they lacked was where she excelled. Dodger would have foreseen any attack. Amelia would be best suited for running the attacker down. Eliza was the only one who could battle him at any range.

All she had to do was keep her eyes on him. His stealth suit made it impossible for her to detect him with her sensus. Its ability to change color made it difficult to see when it was in shadows or against flat colors. It was a tool favored by assassins and thieves of the highest order.

Eliza flung five bolts of pure animus from her fingertips and directed them to arc around, thus making them harder to dodge. He tried ducking into an alleyway but the bolts had ensnared him. They were all going to hit him until he summoned a wall of green flames to block two of the bolts and open up an escape route.

She was losing ground and to keep an eye on him she would need an elevated view. So she opened a water container and swirled the liquid around. This is her favorite way of travel and one that showed her cleverness in manipulating her environment. She used the water to create a series of mobile puddles that suspended her weight in the air. A mage with a more developed animus would be able to create wings of mana to fly. Then there was the cruder method of using telekinesis to throw oneself. She did not have the stamina to sustain either of those methods of transportation for a prolonged period. Condensing water in the air and walking across the sky required far more finesse and control but ultimately required much less energy.

While traveling upwards she found it easier to get a favorable angle on her target. She flipped over and created a disc from her animus and aimed her blade near where the target was heading. She kicked off the disc at great speed aiming herself like a dart while absorbing thermal energy from the air to prepare for her attack. The faster she fell the hotter her body got thus giving her more thermal energy to absorb and turn into a chilled wind.

This energy coursed through her blade–the fabled Moon Piercer–to create a wave of ice and wind that formed a glacier in the street. Jagged edges of the ice sheet slammed into the assailant halting his progress. In retaliation he coated his blade in green flame to cut through the ice wall that had formed. Eliza didn't stop at limiting his movements. As soon as the blade was swung she used telekinesis on a cluster of ice crystals and struck the man in the chest.

"Give it up." Eliza warned as she held her rapier to his face.

"Sorry princess, but I outlasted your predecessors and I'll outlast you as well." His voice was modified by a device on the stealth suit's mask. This man was attempting to conceal his identity. This made Eliza even more suspicious. She knew but one man who both referred to her as a princess and whose mana manifested as green.

Before Eliza could remove his mask to see if her suspicion held water, the assailant tossed a grenade at her. She trapped the exploding grenade in a ball of condensed air. As she was focused on that the assailant dropped a smoke bomb. Her vision was obscured and when the smoke cleared he had vanished.

"Damn it." She cursed under her breath as she looked around for the assailant. He was nowhere to be found, he disappeared within the crowds that had gathered along the seat. Eliza cursed her own lack of preparedness. Had she had her Reflected Sphere Generator on her she could have made it far more difficult to escape. But alas there was only one assigned to her and Amelia had taken it with her on her daily routine.

"Eliza!" Hearing her name shouted with such enthusiasm right after a failure made the arch knight sigh in frustration. She didn't even need to turn around to see who it was. He must have caught wind of the excitement and saw fit to stick their noses in her business yet again.

"What do you want, Dodger?" She turned to face the tall demoran boy and studied him with scrutiny. She knew in the back of her mind that Dodger was not the man she had just encountered but part of her hoped he was.

"I saw the blast and thought I'd come here." Dodger said.

"Is that so?" Her eyes hardened against Dodger. She had never sought his trust. They ultimately worked towards the same goals on more than one occasion but he always brought out her worst competitive tendencies. He had been a thorn in her side ever since taking this position. That thought is what kept her from suspecting him entirely. The last words the assailant said could not have come from Dodger's mouth. "I'm surprised Oliver isn't with you."

"That was my reason for being out and about. Oliver is a little tied up right now. I volunteered to run some errands for him."

"And that just so happened to bring you here?"

"Huh? Shadowbrooke isn't that big." Dodger was sensing the hostility and matching it with hostile feelings of his own. "If you're all torn up about the guy you were chasing just give me a call and we'll catch him next time."

"You don't understand. There is no you in this we. You two need to stay out of my way. Amelia and I don't need you two. We don't need amateurs with no respect for decorum. We certainly don't need vigilantes putting themselves at risk, trying to put their deaths on our conscience. And I certainly don't need help from the likes of you."

"Not my analysis." Dodger teased.

Eliza considered herself a patient person even if she was the only one who would say so. Her patience was flexible at best. Her tolerance for Dodger's presence changed on a day to day basis. On this day it was at its lowest. She had no desire to talk with him any further.

"You have ten seconds to get out of my sight before I'll…"

"Excuse me Princess for not getting in the way of your chase so you could blame me for your failure."

Dodger got a whiff of Eliza's bloodlust at that moment. Even someone who enjoyed agitating people knew better than to push it any further. He also had Oliver to consider. The younger boy looked up to Eliza as a strong and graceful mage. He had a rendezvous to honor and both parties he was going to see had wanted him to stay on favorable terms with the arch knight. And so he took his leave without antagonizing Eliza further or telling her what had happened.

Eliza did find out later that night that Oliver had been captured by some thug. She had half a mind to storm into Dodger's apartment and beat him senseless for that. Yet by the time she had decided on anything a breaking news report said that Oliver Turner was back home safe. The official story was that he had a bad run-in with a criminal while at the park and was found beaten up across town but was making a quick recovery.

What none of the stations knew to report was the manner in which he had escaped. Nor were any stations connecting his day in captivity with the riots that were cropping up across the county or the attempt on Donovan Brown's life. There was only one warrior of justice that was able to see the connection between all three events and that man was someone Eliza didn't know existed.

CHAPTER 20

The Agents Take a Chance

It had been a long chaotic day but it was far from over. Dodger arrived at the Turner's home with food so that the members of Nightwatch could talk things over a meal. It would be the first time he had seen Sir Nightwatch in the flesh in over a year. Billy Turner was sure to be upset with him for getting Oliver into such dire straits. He had also been on and off the phone with Brittany Rembrandt and Rachel Rune to assure them of Oliver's condition.

When he arrived Billy stood up only to be stopped by Sir Nightwatch himself. Oliver was still reeling from his ordeal but was making a quick recovery. Sir Nightwatch was still fully cloaked but had placed his hat on the kitchen counter and made himself comfortable.

"No need to punish the boy Mr. Turner." Sir Nightwatch said as he pulled the concerned father back down into his chair.

"I take full responsibility for putting Oliver in their sights. My only defense is that I correctly predicted they would have no desire to kill him."

"Now, report." The light never left Sir Nightwatch's amber eyes. He was very much like a nocturnal raptor waiting patiently for the perfect chance to strike.

"Eliza Alcius had a run in with the same man I encountered the night we fought the vampyr."

"What man?" Oliver asked. Sir Nightwatch raised a finger to silence his youngest agent.

"Are you sure?" Sir Nightwatch asked.

"Positive. I sensed Eliza battling but I was unable to gauge who she was fighting against. There's only one reason that would be the case and that's that he was using a stealth suit."

"I take it Eliza was responding to the explosion in that campaign office?"

"As far as I could gather she was there when it happened."

"Did she say anything else?" Oliver asked.

"That we should stay out of it. That I was a good for nothing trouble-maker and that if either of us died it would be on her conscience. She was just projecting her own failures onto me as usual."

"Dodger." Oliver disapproved of his mentor's antagonism towards The Celestial Order. Sir Nightwatch on the other hand had come to suspect it.

"If what you said is true then the arsons, the vampyr and the political upheaval are all connected." Sir Nightwatch said. "If we're to get ahead of this situation we're going to need more information. I could probably find one of The Hellfire Brats and make them talk but I take it you have another idea."

"Donovan Brown was one of the first arson victims and he happened to call Eliza the same day that kid got shot and at that same time someone tried whacking him. He knew something and passed that information to Eliza."

"I will look into things to see if anyone else was there." Sir Nightwatch stood from his seat. At the gesture of his hand his hat snapped onto his head from across the room. "After that I'll be heading back to Chicago. They know we're onto them so there's no telling how their plans may change from here. I will keep an eye on the situation from that end."

"You're leaving already?" Oliver asked.

"We all have our part to play. Try to be ready to play yours when the time comes." Sir Nightwatch took his leave without taking a single bite of the food Oliver had brought.

The remaining three people sat and ate. Dodger spent the majority of his time covering for his own failings and trying to ease the tension between himself and Billy Turner. He was on strike two. If he miscalculated again it could result in a fracture in their standing at best and Oliver's death at worse.

Eventually the subject of the conversation changed to Eliza. Oliver was growing increasingly bashful about that subject and Dodger saw fit to tease him about it. It was written all over the boy's face that he had some sort of admiration for the arch knight.

"It's no secret I don't like her and she doesn't like me." Dodger said. "But as much as I hate to admit, she's strong, a great fighter, and a worthy guardian of this area. But she's a lousy detective. She won't know what to do with the information she was given. We should relieve her of it."

"What are you plotting?" Oliver set his food down and gave his partner a disapproving glare.

"I'm just saying that we need some police records to get the dirt we need on The Hellfire Brats and breaking into her place will be easier than breaking into a police station."

"Are you crazy?" Oliver asked.

"Kinda."

"No, I can't agree with you breaking into Eliza's house."

"Oh I'm not going to." His smirk sent a shiver down the younger boy's spine.

"No." Oliver shook my head. He had figured out what was going on in Dodger's head and he was not on board with it.

"Eliza is a celestial knight, an Arch Knight at that. She'll have numerous systems in place that'll cause hell for a demoran like me. But you ...you have human blood. You should be able to sneak in and out no problem."

"This is wrong." Oliver continued to shake his head.

"Look kid, when you want to be the hero you have to work outside the bounds of the law. Nightwatch, our whole operation, if someone like Eliza finds out what we really are, the celestial inquisition will start hounding us. We can't afford to just team up with The Celestial Order. We have to do things ourselves."

"Then you do it."

"I can't. I already told you. I've done it before, she found out, and put a bunch of measures to keep me away."

"You already did it before?" Oliver wasn't even surprised at this point.

"Had to swipe her celestial compass somehow." He shrugged. "I'll be right down the block guiding you through it. Just...trust me."

"I do trust you." Oliver said. "I also trust Eliza and Amelia. I don't want them to think of me the same way they think of you."

"You're already guilty by association in their eyes. Have been since the night we ran into that vampyr." Dodger sighed and scratched his head. "Look, if you want to tell Amelia what we've learned go ahead. There's no guarantee Eliza will believe you and act accordingly. If we get our hands on their information we will act on it. This is our best bet for stopping whatever is going on."

Oliver thought it over for a moment. He looked at his father for guidance. No words were shared between them. As far as Billy Turner was concerned this would be the least crazy thing Oliver would do as an agent of Nightwatch. Oliver also realized that if he succeeded and they brought The Hellfire Brats to justice it may even impress the arch knight.

"Fine." He relented. "I still morally object to breaking and entering. But if this really is our best bet at foiling whatever game The Hellfire Brats are up to, then I'll do it."

That was all he needed to hear. After the sun went down the next day they drove near Eliza's house. While on the way Dodger filled Oliver in on the particulars of Eliza's abode. She and Amelia would be out on a hunt and the only one they needed to worry about was Viggo Pendersen.

The house was fairly large. It had two stories and a fully finished basement. It was the kind of house Oliver would want to live in. There was a sign in the front noting that it was property of The Celestial Order. Only one of the lights were on, upstairs where Viggo's room was. This was the perfect time to sneak in.

Oliver was dropped off down the street. If Dodger was to get any closer he would have likely been detected. From there Oliver snuck around the back and walked up to the nearest window. Luckily, Eliza's office was on the bottom floor. The window into the study was locked just as expected. Oliver first tried taking a deep breath and using telekinesis to unlatch it. He got excited when he saw it wiggle, but then it got stuck. He kept at it for a minute before giving up and calling for help.

"Are you in?" Dodger asked.

"Not yet." Oliver stated.

"What's the problem?"

"The window lock won't budge." Oliver turned on his phone's camera to show his partner what he was talking about.

"Yeah, just one of the defensive measures meant to keep me out." He said. "I was worried she might still have that in place. Fun fact, messing with that lock is how I got so good at telekinesis."

"So it can be done?" Oliver asked.

"Not without a ton of practice. You're barely able to move one mechanism at a time. You have to move three in order to trip that lock."

"Can you do it from where you're at?" Oliver asked.

"Most magic requires line of sight. But with a strong enough sensus, and some careful calculations, you can pull telekinesis on anything. So long as you know exactly where it is." He said. "Clear your mind and I'll divide part of my attention to see through your eyes."

Clairvoyance was something Dodger was still refining. Having the ability to project his psyche and perceive what others could is what made his sensus a level three. He had yet to put that to this rigorous of a test. He saw everything Oliver did as he focused on the young boy. He saw the lock as clearly as he would if he was standing right there. He also knew he had to act quickly. Even if his physical body wasn't there, the presence of this spell was sure to trip some kind of alarm.

After doing some mental math he managed to trip the rest of the lock in conjunction with what Oliver had accomplished. After that he quickly abandoned Oliver's mind and urged him to move forward.

The first thing Oliver came to admire about the study was the sheer amount of books. He always took Eliza as the well-read type but he found this to be insane. *A Full History of The Celestial Order*, *Laws and Legislation of The Celestial Order*, *An Introduction to Magic* and *Men and Monsters of the Demon Realms* all by Ian Aldrich were the largest of the books. But there was also a Bible, various other Christian texts, as well as an entire shelf of Mythology books from across the globe. Then there were several history books, books on music, architecture, business, politics, and animals. Just this glance at her bookshelf told Oliver more about the knight's interests than any conversation they had ever had.

True to form, unless you count religious and mythology texts as fantasy, there was but a single fictional text in the entire study. It was *A Collection of Danish Fairy Tales*. And it was quite noticeably the most well-worn book in the study. This was one book Eliza had ever since she was a child growing up in Copenhagen. At one point she found comfort in this book that she never got from her scattered family. This was the first book

Eliza ever learned to read and here it was years later, sitting next to the kinds of text all celestial knights would have on their shelves.

Oliver refocused on the reason he was there at all. He slowly moved to the desk, careful not to make a sound. It was times like this that it paid to be small. The floor barely made any sound as he shifted his weight across the floorboards. On the desk was a sheet of paper with a red arcane emblem on it. Looking at the symbol made Oliver's eyes water and his skin itch.

"Aah, another one of her anti-Dodger measures." Dodger rang. "It creates this aroma that purposely messes with my senses."

"It's not making me feel good either."

"Well, power through it. You're looking for an envelope. Hurry up and take pictures of its contents."

"Wouldn't it be easier to just steal it?"

"If worse comes to worse, sure. But it'll be really cool and funny if we do this without Eliza ever finding out."

Oliver shook his head as he looked over the paperwork neatly compiled on the desk. At the very top of the left-hand side pile was a file marked "Arson Case." The first few lines confirmed the contents were what he was looking for. There were some transcripts, notes and reports.

He didn't bother reading it. He took pictures of it, page by page. The longer he took the more he sweated. His skin was crawling. His heart was aching. He knew he shouldn't be there. But he was. And he wasn't going to chicken out just because of his nerves.

He kept snapping pictures. He kept feeling worse and worse the longer he took. He thought he was just feeling bad about doing something illegal. He thought it was guilt over violating this room, a room Eliza considered a sanctuary. His hands started to shake and he had to retake one of the pictures because it was too blurry.

"Oliver, best get out of there." Dodger said.

"I'm almost done." He only had a few more pages left.

"You probably have enough. Don't get greedy."

"I can...do this." He took one last picture. His senses were dulled and so he didn't hear anything until the latch on the door clicked.

"Oliver hide!" Dodger screamed.

It was too late. The light flicked on. Eliza had sensed his presence as soon as she pulled onto the street. She was standing there, blade in hand. Her face simmered with a cold anger. Oliver's heart sank. He felt like he could drop dead. He thought maybe that would be for the best. He had been caught red-handed in her office. And he couldn't think of a good excuse. He was once again in a bind and this time he would have to get out himself.

CHAPTER 21

Oliver Interrogated

Eliza had long since given up on preventing Dodger from skulking about her home. After the last time he did such a thing Eliza did not upgrade her security any further. Instead she divested resources into detecting intruders and sending that information to her phone. She had been notified the second the lock was tripped. It had only taken a few minutes for her to get back home. She was however surprised that it was Oliver, not Dodger, hiding away in her office.

She was both disgusted at Dodger for putting the boy up to this and angry at Oliver for going along with it. This went above and beyond the scope of mere freelance monster hunters. They were now actively involving themselves in matters that should only concern licensed individuals.

Before he could even say a word she used telekinesis to pull the headphones out of his head and into her hand and his phone flew out of his pocket along with it. Then came the chill. She drained the heat from the room. Slivers of ice appeared on his arms and head and a chunk of ice covered his leg, trapping him.

"Give me one reason why I shouldn't pulverize you." She said.

"I…I don't have a reason." He admitted with his head hung low.

"Dodger put you up to this?"

"Yeah, but I went along with it." He showed honesty enough to cool the arch knight's attitude. Had he tried to lie she was liable to smack him across the face or slam him into the floor. After seeing the files he had open she decided to look through the photos on his phone. It confirmed her suspicion as to why he broke in.

She had to exert control over the situation. She had been patrolling with both Amelia and Special Agent Clint Finch. The latter of which volunteered for extra manpower in case the assassin tried killing her again.

"Everything alright?" Amelia asked as she walked into the room. "Oliver?"

"Should I arrest him?" Cline Finch asked. "He did break in."

"No." Eliza said coldly. "Mr. Turner here is no one to concern yourself with."

"Are you sure?" He asked. "The contents of that file are sensitive."

"I will conduct official business as I see fit. Oliver Turner is a freelance would-be mage detective. He obviously wants to try solving the case himself."

"Mr. Finch, if I may...Oliver is a good kid." Amelia defended him.

"Not too good to follow the law." Mr. Finch said as he crossed his arms.

"I vouch for him. I've been helping train him. He has potential, and would make a strong ally to The Celestial Order should he choose to join us."

"Exactly." Eliza said. The arch knight did not actually share her partner's sentiments. She didn't see the same potential that Amelia and Dodger had. That actually helped Oliver's case. She wouldn't hand him over to the police no sooner than she would call an exterminator to handle a single rat."Now Mr. Finch, you are dismissed."

"If you say so." He groaned. He gave Oliver one more detested look before heading towards his own vehicle parked out front.

"Amelia, make sure Dodger doesn't try intruding to help him." Eliza commanded.

"Eliza …take it easy on the kid." She begged.

"I will take it under consideration." Eliza kept her voice cool and leveled. "Now leave us."

As soon as she heard the door clicking shut, she withdrew her blade and crossed her arms. She first made him bow and then flung him into the chair. She covered his wrists and ankles with cuffs of ice that trapped him in the chair.

"Ow." He groaned.

"I've been meaning to talk to you." Eliza said as she sat on her desk. She took a more studious glance at the file making sure nothing was out of place before proceeding. "What's your interest in this case?"

"We just want to figure it out." Oliver said. "Dodger, he saw it in the papers and then …we um…we started looking into it."

"And you thought the best way to do this was to break into my home?"

"Dodger's idea. I…I have no excuse. I let him talk me into it."

"This isn't the first time." Eliza sighed recalling a similar confrontation with Brittany Rembrandt. "What is Dodger to you?" It took him a minute to answer the question. Far longer than it should have. Oliver had been asked that question before but had never settled on a satisfying answer. For comparison Brittany had instantly said that she was going out with Dodger when she had butted heads with the celestial knights.

"A friend I guess." He finally replied.

"You don't strike me as the type to be drawn to his antics. On the first day of school he sought you out. Amelia saw your interaction and told me about it later. According to his flimsy excuse, he ran into you the day before. I know that was a lie because that day we were both chasing a shadowy storm cloud that had appeared above Shadowbrooke."

"We must have ran into each other before then." He said. The ice cuffs extended further up his arms in response to the fib.

"You're lying. Those cuffs have microscopic needles digging into your bloodstream and monitoring your heartbeat. Think of it as a crude lie detector." It was a little more complicated than that, and nowhere near as accurate as an actual lie detector. It was most effective against honest fools like Oliver who wouldn't know any better.

"This hurts a lot." He cried out. The small ice needles were keeping track of his heart rate and embedded into his mana. It was a sensation Oliver had never felt before and he couldn't accurately describe the flavor of pain the frosty snare caused.

"The night in question, the storm cloud disappeared. There was a report of someone using a Reflected Sphere in your neighborhood around that same time. I assumed it was a celestial crusader, chasing a monster into the city before disposing of it." It was a likely story. Crusaders were in a similar position as knights yet operated entirely outside the cities. There was an extensive rivalry between the three branches of The Celestial Order and while Eliza had never been notified of such action, the crusaders never denied an operation in Shadowbrooke either.

"I didn't see any crusader." Oliver said.

"But you did see something." Eliza guessed. "The night with the vampyr, that happened the same exact night as the arson that transpired here in Shadowbrooke. Had I not responded to that threat, I would have detected the use of magic nearby and done something about it."

"Why are you telling me this?"

"Because ever since you came into town, something has been brewing. Arsons, assassins, distractions, and right in the middle of all of it has been you and Dodger."

"Do you think I had something to do with this?" He started to choke up. Oliver took offense at the implication that he had done anything wrong, outside of breaking and entering of course.

"No. If you did, you would have destroyed the file instead of copying it. But you do know something. The only reason I have that file is because someone tipped off the police. The only other people looking into this case are you and Dodger."

"I didn't call the police. And I don't think Dodger did either." His voice lowered when he mentioned Dodger because he couldn't say for certain that Dodger didn't orchestrate that event. He had his own ideas though and he would rather not share them with Eliza. She picked up on this hesitance and continued her line of questioning.

"I want to know...what you know." Eliza said as she leaned in and tightened his restraints. "You know something I don't. Dodger doesn't want you to tell me because he doesn't trust me ...either that or he wants the glory of solving this case for himself. Most likely both are the case. Do you trust me?"

"Hard to say when you have me bound up like this!"

"I'll free you as soon as I have something satisfying." Eliza promised.

"Uhh, ahh God Damn It!" He grunted. "The Hellfire Brats. We think it was a gang called The Hellfire Brats."

"Hellfire Brats?" Eliza repeated as she leaned back. It wasn't a name she was familiar with. That meant they were either small or cautious or both. The arch knight found herself biting her nails as she thought through various possibilities.

"Dodger said they're a gang of demorans that live around here. There's only a few of them. We confronted them one night on a hunch. We found out that they received a list of dates and addresses from some guy up in Chicago. I don't know the rest but there's gotta be more to it. One of them even captured me. If it hadn't been for Sir Nightwatch..." He stopped himself before he could say any more. Her interest had already piqued when he mentioned his kidnapping. It was the first Eliza had heard of it. She thought about looking into it later but with Oliver safe it could at least wait until the morning. The other thing he said was far more intriguing.

"Sir Nightwatch?" She asked. That was a name vaguely familiar yet she couldn't place her finger on why it was so. "What does he have to do with this?"

"Nothing." Oliver pleaded. He had spoken out of turn and was trying to get her to forget what he said. It was a futile effort though. Now that the name had reached Eliza's ears she dwelled on it. "Just a name I heard while working with Dodger."

"Nevermind that for now." Eliza filed the name of Sir Nightwatch into the back of her mind and got back to the task at hand.

"Dodger said if he could just look at the contents of that file he would have everything he needs to make a move on The Hellfire Brats." Oliver blurted out.

"Well…" Eliza contemplated her actions. She took his phone, and deleted most of the pictures he had taken but purposely left the pages she had received from Donovan Brown. Her idea was to use them to her advantage. There were at least two forces to reckon with. There was the man in the stealth suit and the gang of demorans. Working in teams could prove beneficial to everyone involved. So long as she could get all the glory she could swallow her pride just this once. "Communication is a two-way street. If Dodger were to have everything, if he has this file, then I have everything now that I know about The Hellfire Brats."

"What are you doing?" He asked.

"Giving you a new angle." She tossed the phone back to him. "I'm only going to tell you this once. Back off the arson case. I was the one who was asked to solve it, and I will. But, I'm no fool. You and Dodger can be of use to me yet. If the assailant I was chasing earlier today is a member of The Hellfire Brats, you have free reign to bring him in or bring him down. Permanently if need be."

With that said, Eliza let him go and ordered him out of the house. Dodger was waiting for him in the front yard. Eliza refused to make any comment towards him. She had a lot to think over. Oliver had also mentioned a man up in Chicago. Deacon Sara Mills was stationed there. She was Eliza's direct superior and the two were on good terms. Eliza planned to ask her directly if she had any useful information about Chicago crime circuits running through St. Louis.

Then there was the matter of Sir Nightwatch. Mulling over that distant yet familiar name she sensed a shadowy specter watching over her and this whole city. Things started clicking in place. Oliver and Dodger's relationship made more sense if it was ordained. No crusader had reported their presence in the night of that stormcloud. She also recalled strange orders she received from her father years earlier asking her to play fair with Dodger. She initially thought it was out of character but then believed that he was only telling her not to look that gift horse in the mouth. Now there seemed to be more to it.

She took the file she kept on Dodger from her filing cabinet. In a big black marker she wrote "SIR NIGHTWATCH?" on the inside fold. Her gut told her to go about this research alone. If she had never heard of this figure before there was perhaps a good reason. Alerting her superiors or the other branches of The Celestial Order would surely make it even more difficult than if she tried heading this quandary herself.

"Lady Eliza." Viggo entered her office. "I apologize for not apprehending the intruder myself."

"It's okay, this encounter works to my benefit." She glanced over at the pudgy old man. His mustache twinkled and the light of the office glistened off his bald spot as he moved out of Amelia's way.

"You didn't have to ice him in the chair." Amelia chastised.

"Don't question my methods." Eliza said as she leaned back in her chair. "Viggo, you've been in service to the order for a long time, have you ever heard of a Sir Nightwatch?"

"I don't believe I have." He shrugged.

"Neither have I." Amelia said.

"Of course. Why would either of you know of such a thing?" She asked. "Yet Oliver knows, Dodger too." She bit down hard on her knuckle. "It's like hearing that name has cast a shadow over everything that has happened the last five years."

"Five years ago was a troubling time for everyone." Amelia said.

"Most of all you." Eliza noted. She could tell her partner was thinking of her parents, who were murdered around the same time the girls graduated. It was only a short time later that Eliza was moved to Shadowbrooke and was made an Arch Knight. Within a month, she had met a twelve-year-old Dodger. Five years later Eliza was sixteen, just about to turn seventeen. And just now she was beginning to question what sort of role she had in this city. She would not stand for anyone getting in the way of her dream to become Grand Priest. Especially not a demon like Dodger.

CHAPTER 22

Dodger at a Protest

One of the dates found on the letter Dodger acquired had arrived. While the address that corresponded to that date was empty there was a gathering of protestors down the street. Dodger had kept and eye on the address all day. Upon a quick inquiry he found out that it was good office space. It was the sort of building that could be used for anything and as such there were several companies bidding on it.

The prior owner had died and the building was left abandoned. There was nothing inside. Not even a single sign of a squatter. Dodger could think of no reason why anyone would want to burn it down. Then again, there were other dates and places that didn't line up with the arsons. Dodger had done his best to dig for information regarding the memo and found nothing cohesive. The closest thing he could think of is that it was a deadline for a deal.

All the listed properties that hadn't burned down were either personal residences or businesses that had been sold. The ones that had burned down were all insured and the money always went to a Chicago-based business. Sir Nightwatch had already surmised the insurance money was being spread around to avoid detection but that didn't explain the residential addresses. The breakthrough came with the file Eliza had received.

The various residents were being threatened. None of them would admit as much but Donovan Brown did. He was offered dirty money from the mob and when he turned it down he was given a deadline to reconsider.

As soon as that deadline was reached his house burned down. Which meant that Sebastian Crane and The Hellfire Brats were just hired thugs making good on the mob's threats.

There was one other matter to consider and one Dodger had to wait on a phone call to clear up. That call came in the middle of the day. The demoran agent answered the phone and was greeted by the voice of Sir Nightwatch.

"Report." His voice was staticky and even. Dodger filled him in on everything he had found after following the leads he had. He then prepared to bring up that other matter to his boss.

"Oliver let your name slip to Eliza." After Dodger spoke there was a brief pause. He sensed no malice or disappointment from the phone.

"It was inevitable." Sir Nightwatch finally answered. "The more Eliza Alcius grows, the more information she will become privy to. Up to and including my existence."

"Even if you did expect it, isn't this premature?"

"That remains to be seen." He added a little chuckle. "The only ones that know of my existence are the current Grand Priest, the other members of the Grand Council that rule The Celestial Order and a few other note-worthy members."·

"I sense some history there." Dodger almost never asked about Sir Nightwatch's past. What little he had gleaned seemed too distant from the man he knew his entire life. If a man did exist before Sir Nightwatch he was undoubtedly an unrecognizably different man than the one who hid in the shadows.

"No one is born into this world fully manifested. Even I have a past. One that was stricken from the record when I became Sir Nightwatch. But even a man such as I, can only hide so much for so long."

"What happens to us when you get dragged into the light?" Dodger's question was met with another pause. It was one that neither of them had paid much thought of until now. Sir Nightwatch had his plans for that eventuality but how to execute those plans depended entirely on how events unfolded.

"All will be revealed in time." Sir Nightwatch hung up the phone leaving Dodger to ponder his own crypticness. This was the first time Sir Nightwatch treated him the same way he had treated his classmates.

The property Dodger had scouted was in the old town area of Shadowbrooke. Cobblestone sidewalks lined the oldest streets in the town. There were tons of shops of all descriptions lining the street but many of them had closed early in anticipation of the current protest going sour. In a few of the smaller ones there were guards posted outside. Families had taken up arms to make sure no protester destroyed what they spent their whole lives building.

Dodger began mingling with the crowd. He was careful not to let any of his own opinions slip. He knew full well the media had whipped these people into a frenzy. It was just rotten timing that the incident with that kid happened the same day Oliver was kidnapped. Unless it wasn't a coincidence. That thought put the demoran at unease. It made him sick to his stomach to think this whole thing was because a criminal wanted more money and power.

The crowd's mind had been made up. They declared the shooting, and the assassination attempt of Donovon Brown, as hate crimes the police were doing nothing about. They were angry. Their high emotions were palpable. Things were bound to escalate no matter what Dodger did. The most he could do was use his powers to nullify as much damage as possible if it came to that.

The best way to stand against the violence came into sharp focus when he picked out a familiar aura within the crowd. One person who was there was bound to make things much worse if things escalated into a riot. Dodger knew above all else he had to nullify this threat.

"Sebastian!" He grabbed the thug's collar and pulled him close. In response Sebastian grabbed the agent's wrist and smirked.

"Easy there Dodger."

"What are you doing here?"

"Ah, Dodger, you know I just love it when a community comes together as a family. Especially when they're doing so to demand justice for the death of one of their own at the hands of an authoritarian regime."

"Don't give me that bullshit Crane. You never cared about humans and you have no stake here in Shadowbrooke."

"Oh but I do. I really do." Sebastian's body began to heat up. He wasn't stupid enough to reveal his powers here in public but as long as their hands were on each other, neither could do anything to change what was going to happen.

The next thing Dodger saw was Michael Corvin. He had slipped in behind Dodger and wound up a punch. Dodger caught a glimpse of the future. The blow would be easy to dodge but if he did, Michael's blow would reach an innocent civilian. If that happened all hell would break loose.

He hardened his corporis and took the blow. As his head reeled forward he caught a glimpse of another figure watching from the rooftops. It was the same man that had threatened Dodger and nearly assassinated Donovan Brown. He was once again wearing the stealth suit and when Dodger tried focusing on identifying the man, Sebastian slipped through his fingers.

The assassin threw a can of tear gas into the crowd. The act of oppression riled them up even more. Within the smoke Sebastian was free to do whatever he wanted. Using the tear gas as cover this time he summoned a violet blaze to his hand and threw it at the nearest building.

Dodger shouted at Sebastian to stop to no avail. Michael tossed the hindrance into the air. Dodger reached out and grabbed the top of a light pole. He caught another glimpse of the future from Michael's point of view.

The Hellfire Brat's toughest enforcer was going to smack Dodger out of the air.

Dodger had just enough time for a counter attack. He turned the entire pole into rubber and bent it backwards. It fired like a sling and at the last second, Dodger returned it to its original material as it batted Michael out of the air.

Dodger's next move was to run to his car. If he was going to fight the demoran brawler he would need a weapon. He emerged from his trunk with an aluminum bat in hand. He took a second to try locating Sebastian but then had to focus all his attention on Michael. Dodger ducked under Michael's punch and swung his weapon only for it to be caught by the thug. Michael Corvin's entire body began to glow a hot red. The heat he conjured softened the bat in a matter of seconds. Before the heat could overwhelm him, Dodger stomped on his foot and used telekinesis on a baseball to strike the demoran across the face. The bat fell out of his grasp and Dodger struck his opponent with a homerun worthy swing.

Michael's corporis was too strong for that to more than stun him. Dodger needed to gain distance and needed to do so quickly. He had but one trick that could achieve that goal. He just needed to solidify particles in the air, increase their elasticity and kick off the air molecules like a trampoline.

It was no easy feet and one that could only be managed by someone with a sensus as fine tuned as his. This traversal trick had numerous applications that made Dodger difficult to fight even for those who outclassed him in nearly every regard.

He kicked off the air three times to gain his distance. He then summoned a baseball to his hand, and tossed it in the air. In an instant he used his knowledge of the surrounding buildings, his impressive physics acumen, and his ability to see seconds into the future to calculate the best trick shot. He slammed the ball and it exploded into green flames. It bounced off a couple walls, increasing its momentum with each collision.

The blow managed to knock Michael backwards and right into the spot Dodger wanted. The air particles around Michael were already suspended by Dodger's previous spell. Turning the air into an elastic semi-solid had proven to be fortuitous in combat. The following technique was one Dodger had learned by complete accident while experimenting with nitrogen atoms. With a single thrust of his fist, a tunnel of air swirled and pushed against itself. It was trapped within the elastic barriers Dodger had created to move through the air. The atoms within that barrier got excited and pushed down the path of least resistance at supersonic speed. This was a technique Dodger lovingly referred to as his elastic air cannon.

Michael had neither the intelligence nor the foresight to harden his corporis in preparation for this incoming attack. The torrent of air pressure ripped his jacket and left a puncture in his chest. He was hit hard enough to break the illusion that made him appear human. This was only the second time Dodger had seen this form and he took the second required to soak it in.

"Rumor has it that demorans from the various bird tribes have it made." Dodger said. Michael's face was shaped like a magpie. Black feathers covered his arms. "Yet the three of you decided to be bums on this side of The Rift."

"What would a member of the goat tribe know?"

"I actually don't care." Dodger answered. "If there's one thing I learned from you assholes, it's that the circumstances of your birth don't matter. I'm going to stop you."

"You'll never stop us." He hissed. "You'll never beat Sebastian so long as you are ashamed of what you really are."

"I am not ashamed." Dodger tore the illusion off his own body. This was the first time Michael had seen this form. Even those who knew of Dodger's heritage had yet to see it. Only Brittany and the members of Nightwatch had the privilege of seeing this under ideal circumstances. The only other one who had seen it was Sebastian Crane.

"Then why fight me?" The voice of Sebastian Crane echoed off the buildings. Dodger spun around and hurled a baseball at the gang leader. It was an insult to think an attack like that would work on the demoran gangster. With a single wave of his hand he incinerated the ball and scattered its ashes into the wind. "Your parents were immigrants from the Demoran homeland. You told me yourself they were killed, just like that kid was killed. You should understand their anger."

"Exactly! That's why I won't let you take advantage of that." Dodger shouted.

"I'm doing what I need to survive!" Sebastian said.

"Damn it Crane." Dodger tried running after him only to be tackled by Michael.

"Things are going to start changing around here." He said as he brushed himself off. "Only way to change is to take control. This city needs a grassroots movement. The only way for grass to take root is to prepare the soil." He summoned a purple fireball in his hand. "Consider this the spark."

With a single wave of his hand he sent a tsunami of flames into one of the buildings. This was not an act of calculation or providence. It was an act of terror. The already rowdy crowd was thrown into panic. Armed citizens revealed their firearms to stave off any attackers. Opportunistic criminals threw bricks through windows. A few men who had been standing by took up arms against the looters and arsonists and became killers themselves.

"Damn it Sebastian!" Dodger struggled against Michael's superior grip. He was lifted off his feet and slammed into the ground. The street melted in accordance to Michael's will and the hot tar burned Dodger's skin. Before he could free himself, Dodger was kicked in the chin by Sebastian who then planted a foot on the mage's throat.

"This could have been our victory. We could burn down this pocket of humanity right now and make our own little slice of hell on Earth. But you just had to try being the hero." Dodger used all his strength to shove

Sebastian off his chest only to be hoisted from the collar by Michael. "Do as you wish Michael."

Michael and Dodger both coated their fists in flames. Dodger was the quicker combatant and connected with a strike strong enough to free him from the brawler. Michael returned to his true form and covered all his feathers in flames. Dodger was not about to engage in a boxing match. Instead he pulled his bat into his hand and started wailing on his opponent. Michael covered his head and waited Dodger out. The Hellfire Brat's champion brawler was far more durable and had far more stamina than the agent of Nightwatch.

As soon as Dodger felt winded Michael pounced and lifted him up into the air. Dodger punched his back as he was carried into an alley and then slammed into a dumpster. He grabbed the lid from the trash can and used it as a shield against the boxer's barrage of blows. At the opportune moment, Dodger changed the lid's chemical makeup to gummy rubber and trapped the brawler's fist. Dodger then leapt back, stretching the rubber lid to its breaking point before letting it go. At the precise moment before the lid smacked his face he turned it back to metal. The aluminum lid struck Michael at a speed nearly as fast as a bullet. Even with his respectable corporis he was still knocked off his feet.

The blow had broken Michael's nose and now that he knew the limits of his durability Dodger could continue swinging on him with his bat. The weapon returned to Dodger's hand yet again as he lined up the strike. Before the metal could meet the mage, Michael molded the concrete of the alleyway to form a defensive pillar. Dodger struck the stone and was rattled by the slab enough to allow Michael back onto his feet. The brawler broke the stone slab and raised it above his head. Dodger narrowly avoided the fatal blow by turning his entire body into rubber and letting the debris bounce off him.

It still hurt and Dodger still had to contend with the goliath looming over him. But that same goliath was now standing where Dodger stood the last time he had leapt backwards. With another empty punch he hit the thug with a point-blank vacuum air cannon that knocked him over and ruptured his ear drums. Dodger took that chance to gain more distance. He used telekinesis to break the nearest wall and pelt his opponent with bricks.

The bricks were far less effective at keeping him at bay than the other blows. Michael was once again on the defensive. His entire body had hardened like diamonds and the bricks crumbled against his skin. Dodger was at his wits end. He had believed that Michael was the easiest of the three Hellfire Brats to beat but he lacked a technique strong enough to break through the trademark hardened skin of a level two corporis. His only hope was that the person he had glimpsed with his sensus arrived before he died.

"I've been waiting for this for a long time." Michael said, sensing the end of the battle approaching. "Traitor."

"Ha, like I would ever seriously consider working with you clowns." Dodger put up a tough guy act. He was running his mouth to stall for time.

"Tough talk for someone in the middle of getting their ass kicked."

"I haven't even begun to get serious." Dodger was bluffing. Not even Michael was going to fall for that. It was all over Dodger's face that he had lost.

"Face it Dodger, you're just a stool pigeon."

"You're the dumbass getting used by some jackoff in Chicago." Dodger laughed. "I wonder what Sebastian would do if he found out I swiped that information right out of your pocket."

"Bastard!" Michael scoffed at the notion. He put his arms around Dodger's throat and lifted him off the ground. Dodger tried hardening his own skin to keep his windpipe from being crushed. He managed to stave off certain death for but a moment. That one moment was all he needed.

"Your next line is… 'What the hell was that?'" Dodger coughed out. Dodger could barely contain his glee as a certain scarlet haired amazonian walked right up behind the bloodlusted demoran and struck him with a punch so hard it cracked his stone skin.

"What the hell was that?" He groaned only realizing an instant later what Dodger had said. The clever demoran slipped from the brawler's grasp as the basal knight sent a hardened knee into the thug's ribs.

Michael turned to face the challenger. Had he not taken so many blows from Dodger this may have been a decent fight. Both warriors had red colored mana and were a class of mage called sonomas–mages who harnessed their corporis before the other tria-ethos. In this situation though, the fight was as good as over. Michael was already worn down and he was little more than a street-tough brawler with some magecraft. Amelia was a warrior trained from birth to make short work of this exact kind of foe.

Michael still gave it a shot. He threw a barrage of flaming punches at the knight but they were all blocked by her shield. Each counter strike left Michael winded. His corporis armor cracked and faded away with each passing strike. Soon all he could do was hope for escape. Amelia was not going to give him up that easily though. She was faster than him and checked him hard enough to knock him onto his face. He then rolled out of the way just in time to avoid a stone splitting stomp.

Michael would have been good as dead right then and there if not for the person who showed up next. Amelia's final blow was intercepted by the man in the stealth suit. He swept the knight's legs and then scooped Michael off the ground.

"You're Copper." Michael's words fell flat as he lost consciousness.

"So that's your name then." Dodger said as he joined Amelia's side.

"I'm a professional, kid. I'm not about to tell a guy like this my personal information." The man said.

"As a knight of The Celestial Order and deputy of the law you are both under arrest." Amelia said as she drew her sword.

"I'm not here to fight you yet." He said as he threw a smoke bomb down. It was composed of a special mineral compound that disrupts a mage's sensus. By the time the smoke cleared he was gone.

"Damn it." Dodger said as he spat out blood.

"Friends of yours?" Amelia asked.

"Michael Corvin of The Hellfire Brats." Dodger said. "Thanks for the assist."

"It was no problem." Amelia looked beyond the alley. The riot had moved out of the neighborhood during the fight. She had run all this way to try and keep people from getting hurt but was too late to do anything besides saving Dodger.

"Where is your boss anyway?"

"Helping the police get things under control."

"Isn't that against protocol?"

"Protocol for her is protecting as many people as she can. And frankly...I wouldn't stand for any less. The Celestial Order has let numerous atrocities befall humanity through inaction. Eliza wishes to end that and I'm going to support her with everything I've got."

"Well, sometimes action isn't the good kind. But, I'm glad the two of you take your own side and try helping everyone rather than picking a side ...and have it be the wrong one."

Amelia and Dodger parted ways after that. Dodger went home to lick his wounds while Amelia helped the police quell the ensuing riot. In the end it was a complete loss for Dodger. He failed to prevent escalation. He failed to stop Sebastian. He failed to take down Michael. He even failed at deducing the identity of the man Michael called Copper. He'd make a vow not to be bested by the thugs again. When next they fought he was going to take them down. He needed Oliver to help make that happen.

CHAPTER 23

Eliza's Letter

Because she was duty bound to help the police all the time Eliza could have spent going after The Hellfire Brats was left cleaning up after the mess the rioters left. For a month straight there was nightly turmoil in the streets of St. Louis. Oftentimes it was accompanied by monsters and on more than one occasion that monster was another vampyr.

Eliza had all but dropped out of school. She rarely even had the time for band class. Lucky for her she had already worked out agreements with the school district to compensate for her work as arch knight. She used to ace tests but now her scores were slipping and her grades along with them.

Viggo and Amelia both tried talking her into slowing things down but the more they reminded her that she was still just a child the more determined she was to prove them wrong. What little sleep she got was plagued with dreamscape memories of her older sister Angelica and her younger sister Penelope. Penelope was currently top of her class in the mage academy. Angelica had also topped her class and made arch knight as soon as she participated in the graduation ceremony and made Deacon as soon as she was eighteen–the minimum age requirement for that position. On top of all her accomplishments as a mage she had achieved such greatness without once letting her grades slip.

Everyone could see it except Eliza herself. She was burning the candle on both ends and on the verge of complete burnout. She was fueled by nothing except toxic amounts of coffee and sheer will power. She had never felt so tired and had never hated the idea of sleeping so much. She couldn't even put a finger on why this case in particular was messing with her mind.

Amelia had been at Eliza's side ever since they were kids. There were three academies run by The Celestial Order. One of them was in Copenhagen where Eliza was born. That's where the pair had met. Eliza was picked on since she was rich enough to inspire jealousy and frail enough to invite bullies. It didn't help that she always felt she had something to prove. If she couldn't at least be as good as her older sister then what good was she? She had been the perfectly wrong age when her parents split. Angelica was five years her senior and was old enough to not let the divorce affect her. Penelope was two years her junior and young enough to not remember much of it.

Various kids looked for any reason to pick on her. They bullied her for her weak constitution, her tendency to get sick, the very public falling out her parents had. It didn't help that at that age she was having immense difficulty learning English as a second language. She cursed those around her for not knowing how to speak Danish. Even all these years later her thoughts were always in that original tongue she learned as a child despite now having a firm grasp of Danish and English as well as German.

Adding to the weight on her shoulders were those above her. Deacon Sarah Mills, all the inquisitors she had reached out to, even her own father had left her to handle this herself. She had sought to type a letter directly to her father to ask for his guidance. All she was asking for was his advice but deep down she desperately needed his approval. She typed up, deleted, rewrote and deleted the message a dozen times over before writing a bland professional piece of mail containing any non-sensitive pieces of information.

After that she tried to relax and take a bath and started winding down from a stressful week. She let the waters soak over her longer than she originally planned. After changing into her nightgown she grabbed another cup of coffee and her laptop. She had her celestial compass active and on the table. She listened to classical music as she got online and refreshed her home page over and over again just waiting for something to break.

Amelia saw this and had grown tired of seeing the person she admired so much destroy herself over things she could not control. She took the coffee away from her boss and closed the laptop in front of her. Eliza's wrathful glare softened when she saw the look of genuine worry on her partner's face.

"You need to sleep." Amelia said.

"I can't." Eliza's voice was softer than a whisper. "The two shield pendants I wear on my collar are a sign of my rank. I was trained to hunt monsters, battle mages and serve as a shield for the people."

"Yes, but if you are to sacrifice yourself, do it on the field of battle, not holed up in your office waiting for something bad to happen." Amelia moved behind the arch knight and massaged the smaller girl's sore shoulders. "If a vampyr attacked right now you would be useless. Wearing yourself thin like this is not doing anyone any good."

"I don't need your worry."

"If you didn't need help they wouldn't have assigned us together."

"Then why are we no closer to catching these criminals? Either you're not good enough or I'm not or both! Which is it, Amelia?"

"It's not a matter of being good enough." Amelia said.

"My sister wouldn't have let any of those demons escape." Eliza's words only lightly scathed the warrior. Unlike Eliza, Amelia took her failures in stride and didn't let them affect her next mission. It was the mentality of a professional athlete Amelia had beaten into herself after years of playing sports. Eliza had never played sports and it showed in how she let every little thing build in her mind.

"You are not your sister!" Amelia put on an angry voice that shocked the arch knight. Amelia had never raised her voice like that before. That shock to the system is exactly what Eliza needed to finally listen to her friend. "You are better than that." The amazon nestled her face into Eliza's blonde locks. "I have absolute faith in you that you can change the world. I will follow you no matter what. But the you I admire so much is not the one sitting here now."

"That's enough Amelia." Eliza said. "I'll go to bed in just a minute." Amelia wasn't fully convinced but knew better than to pick a fight with her now. Eliza needed her support more than ever.

Eliza climbed the stairs and turned down the hall to enter her room. The featureless walls caught the moonlight through the window. It was the room expected of her position as a warrior. The only thing that betrayed the facade was a single stuffed pony sitting on her dresser. This room, which should have been her own private sanctuary, showed less of her true self than her office did. Yet she carried with her a single piece of that true self. Wrapped in her arms was A *Collection of Danish Fairy Tales.*

As she got comfortable on her bed she scrolled through her phone one last time. She decided to reach out to somebody and so she opened up her contacts. She could have laughed at how few numbers were saved into her phone, almost all of them were business related. She also snickered at how she didn't have Dodger's number but somehow had Oliver's. She didn't even remember when that had happened. She scrolled back up to the only M in her contact list. Her thumb lingered over the number for what felt like an eternity before swallowing her pride.

"Hey Mom." Eliza said when it went to voicemail. It was the early morning where Anne Rosen resided as the Paladin of Denmark. As such she was always busy. It had been two years since they had even so much as shared a phone call. Their duties were in such divergent time zones that work never permitted such things. Yet she wanted nothing more than to hear her mother's voice. "I know you must be busy. And it's been awhile since I've even bothered calling you. Sorry about that. I've been busy myself. But I could use some advice. There's these boys, and no it's not like that, this is professional advice. They want to help, but I don't know if I should. Please, call me back when you have the chance. Oh and tell Penelope I said high."

She set her phone aside and opened up her book. She didn't even get past the title page before she collapsed into her sheets. On the first page was a crudely drawn stick figure of a trio of girls. It had been made by Eliza when she first realized she was left handed–the only one in her family to be so. The memory felt so distant that it didn't even feel like the same person. Her heart and eyes were too heavy to make sense of any of the words scribed in both Danish and English. Yes, it was thanks to the translations her mother had scribed within the margins that Eliza was able to first read English. It was a comforting thought knowing she didn't accomplish such a task alone.

CHAPTER 24

Tightening Thread

The Hellfire Brats had set their sights on the backroom of a bar north of St. Louis county. It had been many years since Sebastian Crane had bothered resting in such a small town. Conducting business outside of the usual metro area had one noteworthy benefit. There were less eyes and ears and less chance of anyone knowing this meeting was happening.

Michael and Marcus were both bound in casts after their respective fights. Michael had been infuriated at the rotten timing that robbed him of his victory. Meanwhile Marcus had gone silent. He was still processing what exactly he saw the day he tried using Oliver Turner as bait. Then there was the matter of Copper. Sebastian had met him numerous times over the years yet never once saw his face. He was a well-known entity within St. Louis. He had been something of a boogeyman, only appearing at times of change. He was clearly an agent of the mob but to what capacity nobody truly knew.

Sebastian knew better than to trust someone who was too scared to show their face to their allies. Wearing the mask when dealing with knights and inquisitors was one thing. Wearing it here, where the only patrons were people just as despicable as he was, showed he had no trust in The Hellfire Brats and therefore they should have no trust in him.

"You kids have already cost us a lot of money." Copper said. The assassin was the only one not sitting in a chair. He stood by the door, arms crossed waiting for his employer to arrive.

"Gotta burn money to make money." Sebastian said.

"Well your little punk friend got his ass kicked and now I've had to show myself to every do-good mage in the city."

"I'd like to see you fighting two mages at the same time." Michael said. "You had Eliza Alcius dead to rights and you dropped the ball."

"She wasn't my goal." Copper said.

"Still doesn't change the fact that I've completed everything I have been assigned so far." Sebastian said. "So as far as I'm concerned you are the last person who can judge my boys."

"Now, now, you have all performed admirably." The one who summoned them finally made his appearance. Sebastian had his suspicions about who hired him. He was expecting someone like Francis Puffin to be more hands on with something like this. Instead he was greeted by the same man who introduced him to the wider world of crime. Allistor Briggs was wearing his best suit. And next to him was the one who came up with this scheme in the first place. It was a face Sebastian had seen on TV nearly every day.

"Damien Crow." Sebastian stood to greet his newest guest.

"The pleasure is all mine Mr. Crane." Like his partner, Damien Crow always wore a suit to meetings. They weren't like Sebastian who always wore leather jackets and jeans no matter the occasion or season.

"Mr. Crane." Allistor Briggs spoke up. "We have grown concerned with how much information this Donald Rodgers has gotten ahold of. Have you any idea how many business owners, politicians, cops and journalists we had to pay off and blackmail to make this work?"

"No and I don't give a flying shit." Sebastian said. "Talk to your guys up in Chicago if you want to bitch about too many people finding out what you're up to."

"You and Dodger used to be friends though." Allistor Briggs said as he readjusted his glasses.

"Now, now, no need to suspect the boy." Damien Crow put a hand on the demoran's shoulder.

"Mr. Crow I am here to articulate some of the concerns my boss has had from the very beginning. I meant no offense. If Sebastian Crane is worth what we are paying him I'm sure he is capable of defending himself."

"No offense taken." Sebastian said. "Dodger is a demoran. We ran together when we were kids. Things were different back then. When I found out he was a snitch I burned that bridge."

"Will you be capable of killing him if need be?"

"Willing? Yes. Able…hell yes." Sebastian chuckled. "Dodger is a small fish in a mighty river. He's only gotten this far out of luck. The ones you need to worry about are the knights."

"We have means to take care of that." Damien Crow nodded towards Copper. "Three mages against the four of you should be no problem."

"Four mages." Copper corrected. "Though if you don't count the blonde kid I can hardly blame you."

"You're all wrong." All eyes went to Marcus. This was the first time he had spoken all day. "Eliza, Dodger, that Oliver brat, they're all just dumb kids who are way out of their depth."

"And there you have it." Damien Crow cheered. "Always take the word of your best psychic in these situations."

"I know that better than you." Sebastian said blankly. "And that wasn't a reassuring tone."

"There's someone else watching things. He's the one who rescued Oliver Turner. When I fought him the only thing I could see was my death over and over again. The man who fights in the shadows is not to be trifled with."

"Shadows?" Damien Crow's curiosity had been stoked.

"He's here?" The voice of Allistor Briggs was shaken at this revelation.

"Don't worry Mr. Briggs." Damien Crow said. "Your boss prepared for such an inevitability. That's why I'm here in person."

"Are you telling me you're a mage?" Sebastian asked.

"Why yes I am." Damien Crow demonstrated his powers by summoning a black fireball. "Blackfire News wasn't a name I picked at random. Like you, I had to teach myself everything there is to know about the mystic arts. It's why I understand you. St. Louis has no organization to its underworld. It is anarchy. Everything we have had you do was to make way for a higher class of criminal operations. And I believe you have what it takes to be the ruler of that kingdom of crime."

"Why me?" Sebastian liked the idea of being a big shot crime boss but he was skeptical of the journalist's flattery.

"Because you are one hell of a mage. And you care deeply for your brothers." He pointed to the other members of The Hellfire Brats. "They've both put their lives on the line for you. If that's not loyalty, I don't know what is."

"We've only ever had each other." Sebastian shrugged.

"And whose fault is that? This world has ostracized your kind, punished them for crimes they didn't commit, shoved them to the margins of society. Made it to where they had to turn to crime just to put food on the table."

Sebastian mulled over the words and got a glimpse of the bigger picture. If demorans had to turn to crime, and he was the crime boss, then he'd be directly responsible for them and would be able to create whatever kind of safe haven for demorans he wished. It was tempting from the financial angle and the moral angle.

"You don't have to sweet talk me. I was already in." Sebastian said with a grin. "Just tell me what all I need to do."

"In three day's time all the paperwork will be finalized. We will own this city." Mr. Briggs said. "And there will be no paper trail for them to follow."

"I will safeguard the data transfer." Damien Crow said. "Anyone who comes after me will be crushed."

"The Celestial Order will have their hands so tied up with our pets." Allistor Briggs said. "Copper will tail the knights and kill them when he gets the chance."

"Roger." The assassin said.

"I will leave Dodger to you then, Sebastian Crane." Damien Crow was putting a lot of faith in the man to do his job. Yet however much faith he had in his subordinates, he had twice as much in himself. He needed that much for he would soon find himself in the crosshairs of that mysterious entity known as Sir Nightwatch.

CHAPTER 25

The Agents Prepare for Battle

Oliver Turner had been grounded after his kidnapping. A month passed before Billy Turner had let his son do anything aside from school. He hadn't made a big deal of it when Sir Nightwatch was at their house but he had been furious. He also knew that Oliver would get stronger.

As a father he was at an impasse. He knew how important it was that Oliver trained. He knew even more than Oliver himself did. He and his wife always knew that he would have to join this part of the world eventually. They kept him away from it as long as they did for a reason and it was that same reason that forced him to relinquish his control over Oliver's life. He was an agent of Nightwatch now. There was nothing he could do.

That did not mean Oliver could do whatever he wanted. Sir Nightwatch had made it clear that so long as he lived under his father's roof he had to honor the rules. His punishment for getting kidnapped was to get grounded for a time. Once Billy Turner was satisfied he allowed Oliver to have company so long as that company did not include Dodger. Cutting off contact between the agents was the punishment for both of their negligence.

Eventually that sentence was carried out and the two were allowed to continue their training. Dodger had taken it to heart and watched Oliver like a hawk. He was also not alone in this endeavor. Rachel Rune blamed herself for the situation Oliver had been in and also stuck by the boy even more than she had before. Those who didn't know better began spreading rumors about the duo, but neither one of them acknowledged one way or the other. They knew what was going on and that was enough. It wasn't anyone else's business.

It did make conducting business difficult. Rachel was still keeping secrets of her own. Dodger had figured things out on his own but wasn't going to tell Oliver. It simply wasn't his information to share. He assured his partner that Rachel would tell him everything in due time. In the meantime, Dodger also made sure to let Oliver know what Rachel and her sister knew. They did not know about Sir Nightwatch but they knew everything else. They even knew the things about Dodger that Dodger hadn't felt necessary to share.

One day Oliver, Dodger, Rachel and Brittany all walked to Dodger's house together. The demoran wasn't used to having house guests but he figured he had more space than anyone else in the group. They were originally planning on spending the evening helping Oliver get better control of his powers. That plan changed when Oliver felt another presence inside. The lock on the door hadn't been tampered with. Nothing was out of place. There was only one person it could have possibly been. Sure enough that figure stood over the fireplace, hat in hand, watching the fire eat away at the kindling.

"I thought you said nobody else would be home." Brittany said.

"I thought so too." Dodger admitted. "Is it that time Old Man?" The man in question looked over at Dodger. He remained silent and the silver scarf he wore hid the devious smile across his face. Dodger was unsurprised but Oliver grew nervous about this meeting.

"Hey girls, I think we're not going to be able to hang out after all." Oliver said.

"Well then if it's all the same to you, we'll make ourselves at home." Brittany said. She urged Rachel out of the room despite the smaller girl's protest. She had a better sense of what was going on. "Just let us know if we can do anything to help."

"That won't be necessary." Dodger said.

"Don't be so sure about that." The figure finally spoke. "A battle is on the horizon. I will be staying in St. Louis for the next few days. Only when Damien Crow is dealt with, and The Hellfire Brats are defeated, will I leave."

"Look, I know Sebastian and his cronies aren't a walk in the park but, does this really require someone of your level?" Dodger asked.

"Best to take precaution. The reason why all of this has been going on in the St. Louis area, was to make room for a new center of crime."

"Why would they use St. Louis of all places?" Dodger asked. "New York and Chicago too big for them now?"

"Since I've been working in the shadows I've slowly done what The Celestial Order can't. I've torn apart the crime syndicates. They've been running scared. I've done well to hide my existence thus far but now they're trying to start organizing a syndicate here in St. Louis. I simply can't allow that."

"We should tell Eliza and Amelia what we're planning." Oliver said.

"Don't rely on their help." Sir Nightwatch warned. "As righteous as they may be...their hands are tied by the threads of legality."

"So we're on our own?" Dodger said. "Good, I miss watching you work."

"The one thing that concerns me is Damien Crow. When I went to see the man for myself I saw that he has a large mana pool. He's trained in the ways of magic. I know not how much of a threat he may pose on his own so it is best to deal with him myself. That leaves The Hellfire Brats to you two and whatever help you can scrounge up."

"Wait, we are talking about Damien Crow, the news guy, right?" Oliver asked. The response he garnered was a simple nod. "Great, is anyone else on TV secretly a mage?"

"Roughly ten percent." Sir Nightwatch said. "That's how many mages are in this world."

"My dad is going to kill me." Oliver sighed. "He still thinks I'm not ready."

"And what do you think, Oliver Turner?" Sir Nightwatch asked.

"I want to fight." Oliver said. "If things are really going down then people are bound to get hurt. If you believe this is our one chance to take them all down I will follow you. I'll deal with whatever punishments my dad has in store after that."

"Then it is not just your potential you inherited from your mother." Sir Nightwatch said.

The conversation was not a private one. Rachel and Brittany were both eavesdropping on the conversation from the other room. Sir Nightwatch was well aware of the two girls and what their own inheritance was. Dodger didn't even have to tell him. It wasn't his secret to tell. It's just that such things never went unnoticed by Sir Nightwatch.

Brittany was the more intuitive of the two and could feel Sir Nightwatch's gaze. She was beginning to understand what Dodger had really been doing. She also knew that if Dodger was putting her life on the line then she could too. She wouldn't do anything as foolish as going after The Hellfire Brats but protecting her neighborhood from any monsters the mob would unleash was her duty as someone who could fight. This was her city too.

The only thing holding her back was Rachel. The younger girl clutched her sister's jacket tightly. Brittany knew that look all too well. It was the same look she had every time Brittany would go out on her own. The younger athlete was pleading with her older sister not to get involved.

"I know my limits." Brittany said. "Mom would want me to do everything I can."

"That's what I'm afraid of." Rachel whispered.

The tender moment was interrupted when Dodger walked in the room. Sir Nightwatch had vanished from the premises and the agents were preparing for battle. Dodger grabbed a duffle bag and stuffed it with supplies: a first aid kit, a pair of baseball bats and a dozen balls. He opened his closet and picked out a flame resistant vest for Oliver. Both of them readied up with guns, pads and knives. He then handed a rifle to Brittany.

"You know reading my mind is an invasion of privacy." She teased as she took the gun from his hands.

"I trust you to do the right thing." Dodger said. He looked over to Rachel but never handed her a weapon. "Now trust me to take care of this." Rachel gave up on protesting any further. Nothing she could say would have changed what was bound to happen.

CHAPTER 26

The Night of The Hellfire Brats

Eliza was laying in bed when her celestial compass began beeping. She shot up from under her sheets and quickly put her usual combat attire on. Her outfit was a blend of style with enough practicality to keep her able to move freely. She put her hair up in a ponytail, popped the collar of her coat up, made sure her skirt fit right and completed the set with fancy boots. It only took her a few seconds to prepare, plenty of time to intercept whatever monster had popped up on her radar.

So when she saw that no less than five simultaneous incursions had manifested, her heart sank. The Gateway Arch was built to keep these sorts of simultaneous incursions from happening. That can mean one of two things: either the Arch was broken–which would signal a full-scale invasion by a demoran army–or the scents that her compass had detected were the result of humans releasing monsters into the city on purpose.

Amelia had yet to return home from her errands. Eliza's first order of business was to get a hold of her partner and tell her where to go. She knew far more about the celestial compass and how it worked than Dodger did. All she had to do was look at it and do some simple math to know where each incursion had been detected. She sent Amelia the approximate addresses of four of the incursions and said she would be heading to the fifth herself.

She didn't have time to wait for a response. A siren was ringing all across the county and so Amelia would already be springing into action.

This did put Eliza in a bind. She did have a car but she hated driving. Amelia usually handled all that stuff.

She got situated in her car which was expensive and befitting of a woman of her inheritance. She hooked up her phone and called her partner to get a better handle on where exactly she was at.

"Amelia!" Eliza shouted as soon as she answered. "What is going on?"

"We've spotted vampyrs all over downtown St. Louis and Shadowbrooke." Amelia said. "We're trying to chase them down and contain them."

"Any fatalities?"

"We've lost three police officers." Amelia said.

"Damn it. Get Finch on the horn, tell him to mobilize all police personnel. I want every single person who has a gun and knows how to use it to be out there containing those things."

"Eliza, this isn't Denmark. This is America, we have more guns than people."

"Then tell them to lock the doors and be ready to defend themselves if need be."

Eliza's lip curled inward as she bit her thumb. The county had drills to rehearse for these situations but they were sporadic. Everyone knew to stay indoors but sometimes that wasn't enough. This was a disaster in the making and one that couldn't come at a worse time. They didn't have the manpower to counter such an offensive. Few cities did. Eliza realized that, but at the same time she couldn't help but revel in the possibility of handling this herself. If she could pull it off those stuffy old fools who run The Celestial Order would have no choice but to acknowledge her.

"Eliza, I'm calling Dodger." Amelia said.

"I'm sure that won't be necessary to get him to fight. But tell him to head to the signal south of Forest Park, towards the train tracks. We'll head over to meet them once we have everything else under control."

"Alright, over and out." Amelia hung up.

By the time Eliza arrived at the nearest signal the streets had completely cleared. Judging from the scattered half-empty bottles they must have left in a hurry. There was a donut shop on the street ahead which was the only building that still had its lights on.

Eliza parked her car and took her sword in hand to investigate. Thanks to her sensus she was able to see the monster before it leapt from the roof to attack. It was a vampyr, but not a typical one. The parasite was latched onto the head of a sasquatch. The beast stood eight feet tall and was covered in reddish-brown fur. Its posture was slumped over a bit as the arachnid-like vampyr sent signals to its muscles causing it to move sporadically.

Eliza wasted no time using her animus to blast the ape-like monster with a handful of energy bolts. The monster tumbled over and rubbed its face, sniffling, giving the arch knight ample time for her next attack. Absorbing energy from the air was yet another simple technique novices learned to turn water into ice. The range of this ability increased dramatically once a mage learned to absorb pure mana. This was one of Eliza's strongest abilities and what signaled that she had a level three animus.

The full extent of her blade pierced the ape's stomach. Its blood froze and ice sheaths sprung from its body. Within a second it was completely encased in ice. The monster was trapped but not yet destroyed. She would need to strike it one more time to finish the job and so she prepared a swift and mighty strike. Sparks crackled from her fingertips as she controlled the pressure of the atmosphere around her to summon an electric storm. The wave of electricity blasted the frozen ape, sending vapor and ice flying into the air.

"Ms. Alcius." Her attention was drawn to the radio in her car. It only held her attention for a moment but it was a moment too long. "This is Officer Claymore, where are you?"

"Old town Shadowbrooke near Hamilton Street."

"Hamilton Street?"

That exchange, however brief, opened Eliza up for an attack. She was knocked off her feet by an orange explosion. Her corporis was strong enough to absorb any damage but she had still gotten the wind knocked out of her. There was a second monster, a very particular type of fire spitting ogre called a dzoavits. It too had the vampyr parasite lodged into its eye. It stood over the broken body of the sasquatch and began tearing into the ape's flesh. Blood and sinew sprayed out of the cold tissue as the dzoavits cannibalized it. The ogre ate the ape, vampyr and all. Thick fur–the same color as the sasquatch–coated the ogre's scaly body and he doubled in size.

Eliza was held aloft by her sword. She cursed the very nature of this fowl creature from under her breath. As much as it disgusted her, the instincts of the vampyr proved beneficial. It found the corpse of its brethren far more appetizing than the petite mage it should have been more focused on.

Hand in the air she used the second level of her animus to conjure a weapon large enough to vanquish the ogre. The mighty spear of pure mana was connected to her own body through cables of energy she could control through telekinesis. Such a weapon would be impossible to dodge and by the time the monster even took notice of her, the weapon had already pierced through its shoulder and severed its arm.

Eliza rushed forward hoping to use the enchantment of her blade to finish the job. The dzoavits was not finished yet though. Lava spewed from its mouth forcing Eliza to slow her approach and take to the sky. What remained of the ogre's logic must have taken over because the beast leapt into the air and swatted Eliza back down to the ground.

The arch knight needed not to glimpse the future to know what the monster would do next. It fell from the sky with its mouth hung agape ready to swallow her whole. The mage's only retort was to change the shape of the street to form a barrier of spikes and let the monster impale itself.

The dzoavits did not fall fast enough for the spikes to pierce its skin. Instead it just slid off the defensive structure and right into Eliza's next attack. With her right hand she conjured the gauntlet of a giant to grab the beast and pin him down. With her left, she drove Manegennebore directly into the vampyr core embedded in the ogre's eye. The skull cracked from the inside and its entire brain melted from the pressure built up by the fabled Moon Piercer's enchantment. What fire remained in its stomach vomited up and licked Eliza across the face. The whole beast then exploded in a sporadic display of fire and ash signaling its demise.

With the two monsters dead Eliza returned to her car. She would take another lap around this area to see if there were any more monsters in that incursion group. She also needed to make contact with Clint Finch and see what he was doing at a time like this.

"I could have used some back up." She said into her radio. "Meet up with me when you get the chance."

"Special Agent Finch said you were on Burr Road." Claymore said.

"Burr?" Something was wrong. It wasn't like Finch to make an error like that. "What's the situation?"

"Something definitely came through here but it's quiet now. I'm on my way."

As soon as Captain Claymore ended the transmission Eliza was greeted by another sasquatch. This one was smaller than the last one but it was no less dangerous. It rushed towards Eliza and tackled her into her car. Eliza rolled out of the way of its punch and blasted it in the back. The ape responded by lifting her car high above its head ready to destroy her best mode of transportation and she along with it.

"Oh no you don't." Eliza grunted.

She conjured two discs and threw them at the sasquatch's wrists. They cleaved through the carpal bones and the full weight of the car struck it in the head. While it was pinned, she stabbed downward, destroying its head and burning the body.

It wasn't enough though. She needed to destroy the vampyr core to finish the job. The sasquatch shrugged her off and flailed around the ground. Flesh and blood pulsated from its shoulder as a mass of snakes sprouted from its neck and wrist stumps. The snakes hissed in unison and all eyes were on the lone mage. Just then, a police car came burning down the street.

The full weight of this car crashed into the chimeric monster. Not one to waste providence, Eliza used telekinesis to hurl the mass of flesh into the air. She then summoned an armada of animus bolts and sent them all to eviscerate the monster. She controlled each one of them like a puppet master controlling strings and by the time the monster hit the ground it was little more than a pile of charred flesh and muscle.

"Need a lift?" Captain Claymore said as he climbed out of his vehicle.

"Perfect timing." Eliza said as she stabbed what remained of the vampyr and popped it like a balloon. With the sector cleared she checked her celestial compass. There was another cluster of signals all swarming together. She knew just from their formation that they were stygian birds. They were a eusocial flock of avian monsters that showed up in North America and Europe quite often.

"Just drive." Eliza said as she jumped onto the roof of the police car. "And head southeast."

"Um...are you sure?"

Her reply came in the form of a layer of ice covering the roof and her feet up past her ankle. He nodded and fired the car back up before flooring it in the direction she asked. Right on target, Eliza's strong mana was like catnip for the stygians. They were more like pests than actual monsters and usually ignored normal people in favor of anyone with significant mana. Whoever had unleashed these creatures did so for the express purpose of battling the mage.

Eliza fired a barrage of animus bolts to hit as many of them as she could. Next she summoned an animus forcefield. The beaks of these birds were as strong as bronze but not strong enough to overcome the mage's defenses. They killed themselves smashing against her forcefield.

"Alright, get to the train tracks south of Forest Park." Eliza ordered.

"Can do." He said.

He made a turn down the road and started heading to the highway. As they approached the exit, a green fireball intercepted them. Eliza couldn't react in time. There was nothing Captain Claymore could do to stop it. The tire was blown out. The car started to flip. Eliza freed herself just in time to not be crushed against the pavement. She then used telekinesis to pull Captain Claymore out of the driver's seat. Then, another fireball hit the car and it exploded, sending the two of them spiraling to the ground.

"How come every time we meet things explode?" Captain Claymore groaned.

"Can you move?" Eliza asked.

"Yeah."

"Amelia, we're near the highway and can use a lift." Eliza said but there was no response. "Amelia?" Eliza tapped the device. "Damn thing." Her phone was broken in the crash and therefore she had no way of contacting anyone else.

Eliza still had complete control of her situation. From the time she saw the green fireball she had already begun making preparations. The heat of the car crash replenished the strength she had lost fighting the vampyrs. She extended her own awareness to the ground waiting for the quiet steps of an assassin to shift its weight on the concrete. The various lights made it much harder to maintain the nigh invisible form and Eliza didn't need to see the future to know where he was most likely to strike.

She felt his foot on the pavement. The killer's intent was palpable. The small amount of mana she released into the air collected onto his suit like dust on an unopened book. There was no more hiding from her. For the first time ever, she could see the future. She saw the actions he imagined in his mind. He was going to ram his knife between her shoulder blade and then burn her to a crisp. She would not allow that to happen. Now that she knew what he planned to do, she could stop him.

She turned just in time for a mutual strike. Her left hand snatched his wrist, causing him to miss his mark. She then unleashed all the energy she had been building up into a single electric blast that fried any piece of technology he may have had on his person. She then tore off his mask but before she could see who it was, he was back on the offensive. He was faster and far larger than she was and had much more experience fighting people up close.

He quickly regained the upper hand and blasted her with a beam of concentrated mana. The blow punctured her corporis and left a mark on her skin. Had she been a little weaker the blow would have ran her all the way through. That gave her an idea. She seized control of her organs and caused her heartbeat to slow as she collapsed onto the street.

"Well, well, well." The assailant said. As she laid there on the street she could finally see the face of the man who had caused her so much trouble. "Not so tough are you?" Even if she hadn't removed his mask, without the voice changer his identity would have been clear. It was a voice she had heard countless times. The assailant was Special Agent Clint Finch!

CHAPTER 27

Oliver's Golden Glow

Dodger kept one hand on the wheel and the other on his pistol. The celestial compass had lit up earlier and the agents of Nightwatch were hot on the trail of one of the incursions. Thanks to the tip off from Eliza they wasted no time in tracking it down. Neither one of them had dealt with this kind of situation before. Both boys were scared but had to fight through that pain to do the right thing.

"Oliver, top of that building." Dodger said as he slowed down.

"I see it." Oliver said.

The creature in question had a fleshy body, large leathery wings and a snake in place of one of its arms. Oliver aimed down the barrel of his pistol and fired. The bullet missed its mark so Oliver recalibrated and fired again as Dodger tried matching the monster's speed.

"Oliver!"

"I'm trying!" The car continued to swerve too much for him to hit his mark. He had been to the shooting range a few times and had gotten decent enough to hit stationary targets.

"Just take the wheel." Dodger said.

"I don't know how to drive!"

"Just keep on the gas and don't hit anything." He used telekinesis to keep things going while they made the switch. It was times like this that it proved advantageous to own a convertible.

The car swerved as he jumped out of his seat and onto the hood of the car. In a burst of flames he revealed his full demoran form. Using telekinesis he summoned Oliver's gun from the passenger's seat and took aim. The first bullet ripped through one of the vampyr's wings. The second tore through its legs, causing it to fall to the ground.

Dodger signaled for Oliver to stop the car so they could pursue the creature on foot and make sure it had died. The wheels screeched against the road and Dodger was instantly thrown off the hood. He landed on his feet in front of the car and put his hands out to stop the vehicle as it slid on the road.

"Not like that!" He shouted.

"You told me to stop."

"Just pull over to the side of the road. We can take it on foot from here."

Dodger tossed the gun back to Oliver as he prepared his arsenal. They were near the metrolink station which was usually a busy location. It was different this time. This was the first time either of them had seen the city streets so dead. It was unsettling. Most of the lights were off. It was freezing yet Dodger seemed un-bothered by it. His corporis and choice of gear kept him from succumbing to the weather. Oliver on the other hand was already feeling numb from riding in the roofless car while it was so cold.

"There's something around the corner." Dodger whispered. He took a ball from his pocket and bounced it. With a back hand throw it hit the ground, the nearby wall and then something else.

A large boar the size of a bus charged out of the alleyway. The vampyr core had infected its eye socket and drove the beast to insanity. It sniffed the air and stomped its feet as it looked for a foe to crush. Dodger tempted it with a piece of sulfuric bait. As soon as the boar laid its eyes on the demoran it squealed and rushed him. Dodger raised his bat and adjusted his feet just like a professional ball player. Then just as it was in range, he swung the bat with all his might and blasted it away.

While Dodger was preoccupied with the boar, a second much smaller creature limped its way onto the scene. It was the same vampyr as before. Its severed wing had yet to heal and the leg Dodger had shot was replaced with that of a rat. Beyond that the core of its body was undoubtedly human. The vampyr had covered its face just like the first one Oliver had ever encountered.

Oliver's heart pounded as he emptied his clip into the creature. Sweat built up beneath his outfit. For every bullet hole a snake sprouted to fill in the wound. Time slowed as the monster shoved him against the car. Acidic saliva dripped from its maw. For a moment Oliver felt useless. He had once again failed to kill the creature before it had its claws on him. Then he took a breath and remembered everything he had experienced so far. He plunged the poison knife he had received from Sir Nightwatch into the creature's sternum. That momentary lapse gave him enough time to focus. Light began to cover his vision. He had done it unconsciously against Marcus Kingfisher. Now he was getting a feel for using his animus whenever he wanted.

The monster had gone limp from the blast. Its entire head had been reduced to ash. Oliver gazed upon his hands and could feel the energy coursing through his veins. All he had to do was concentrate on this feeling and he could release the energy in whatever manner he saw fit. As practice, he raised a single finger and aimed it at the boar. A smaller, more concentrated bolt of energy fired from the tip of his finger and carved a path through the back of the boar.

"Nice!" Dodger said as he wrestled the boar to the ground. It wasn't dead yet. From the wound on its back sprouted the tentacles of an octopus that snatched Dodger up. "Oh boy, I've seen this hentai before."

Dodger covered his body in flames and fired his own animus at the bundle of tentacles. Meanwhile Oliver aimed the palm of his hand at the creature and fired a wide beam of energy. The potency of which burned everything in its path away. Dodger tumbled to the ground with the last twitching tentacles of the monster still untouched.

"I did it!" Oliver cheered.

"Yeah boy! We gotta work on your control a bit but that was a damn fine attack."

"That was my animus ethos right?"

"Bet your golden ass it was." Dodger said. "Animus is the first ethos you've tapped into. It's raw pure mana made into a weapon. And yours is even stronger than ...well Sebastian's when we first met." The praise was a grim reminder of what they were truly up against.

"We should get going." Oliver nodded.

"Wait, we should take a breather, aren't you tired?"

"No." He replied.

"Well either you're lying, the adrenaline got to you, or you are way stronger than I first thought you'd be."

"I feel great." Oliver said. Whether he was strong or not didn't matter. The adrenaline of the situation was enough to keep him ready to go.

"You'll make a fine caster yet. Just a shame you couldn't be a psychic like me. It's going to be difficult for me to train you from here on out."

"I'm sure you'll think of something." Oliver shrugged.

After Dodger caught his breath he led the way to the tracks. There was a train there, loading up cargo. As soon as the boys got close, Dodger grabbed Oliver and pulled him away. A wave of purple flames covered the road, cutting them off from the train. As the fire rose three figures emerged from its inferno.

"Glad you can make it." Sebastian said. He, Michael and Marcus were already in their full demon forms. They had predicted that Dodger would take this path and they were ready to burn him down. "I was hoping against hope that you two would be the first to arrive."

CHAPTER 28

Eliza Alcius and the Contradictions of Duty

Special Agent Clint Finch had served The Celestial Order for over fifteen years. He had been in the pocket of the mob for over twenty. He learned all about magic from watching various knights aid the police in dealing with rogue mages. With the help of some deep pockets he turned all that experience into the skills of an assassin. And he did so right under the nose of The Celestial Order.

Eliza lied on the ground in front of him, just another spoiled brat who thought she was better than anyone else because of her position. Clint Finch could do nothing but laugh at the tired joke that anyone could act all high and mighty when they were assigned a city as run down as St. Louis. The police liaison was tired of kowtowing to these mages. If he could pull this job off and escape with his reputation intact he would be able to afford a house in a more respectable city like Miami or San Francisco.

"Out of all the knights I've worked with you were by far the most annoying." He said as he kicked Eliza onto her back. She was still alive but her breath was faint. Just a little more and she would be dead. Then his job would be complete. "Let's see how many bullets your corporis can take." His thumb slowly pulled the hammer of his revolver back. It would be so easy to just put a hole in her head but he wanted her parents to be able to recognize her.

He aimed the barrel of the gun towards the arch knight's petite chest. His gloved hand slowly began to squeeze the trigger and then the echo of a gunshot rocked through the streets. But it was not from the assassin's revolver. A bullet fired from the gun of Captain Johnathan Claymore had found its mark and tore through the turncoat's shoulder. In response Clint Finch whipped his revolver and fired three shots at the cop. All three missed their target and he was forced to retreat behind cover he made out of the street's pavement.

While the assassin was preoccupied with Captain Claymore, Eliza launched her plan. She hit the assailant with a small, sharp, almost imperceivable slice of wind that tore clean through his side. Panicking, he launched a green fireball at the arch knight and watched in rage as she caught the fireball in her hand. Its green flames faded to blue and then she took the burning energy into her own body to replenish her own stamina.

"You're going to have to try a lot harder than that to beat me." Eliza taunted. The ability to absorb incoming attacks like that was indeed rare among those of her rank. It was the technique associated with a level three animus and it required the one absorbing the attack to have a stronger ethos than the attacker. "It's best you give up now, traitor."

"Oh, traitor is such a misnomer." Clint Finch mocked with a shrug. "Traitor implies I was ever on your side."

"How long?" Eliza asked.

"Always. At least since before poor old Harrison McCree died. Had to ...tie up that loose end as soon as possible. As for Jeremy Dogget ...didn't even have to kill that dumbass. Chris Crimson did that for me."

To so casually mention two arch knights who once held the same position as Eliza and died in the line of duty was a grave mistake. Eliza had never met either of these men but she knew they had a respectable reputation. They had been good honest men through and through. Chris Crimson on the other hand was a monster so vile even Hell branded him as a creature of evil unworthy of them. By associating himself with that fiend, Clint Finch was tempting Eliza to kill him.

"So that's how it is." Eliza shut down the emotional parts of her brain. Her eyes began to glow with a storm furious enough to pierce the very heavens.

"And you want to know the best part? Your order won't even let you kill me without a formal inquisition. If only I was a demon like your friend Dodger." He laughed.

The sound of gunfire cut off his laugh. Captain Claymore had reloaded and was back on the offensive. Clint Finch created another wall of stone to keep the cop at bay. He then threw a fire bomb into the air in Captain Claymore's direction. Eliza quickly gathered and froze all the water molecules around her and launched the ice blast directly into the fireball making both explode into a hail of water and vapor.

"Stay back." Eliza ordered.

"With all due respect I don't take orders from you." Captain Claymore said. "That man nearly killed me twice." He reloaded his pistol. "He works with police officers but his allegiance is to the criminals we're supposed to stand against. I can't stand here and let him get away."

"Your compliance isn't necessary." Clint Finch mocked. He launched another, more powerful fire blast at the arch knight. He was underestimating her but even still Eliza wasn't going to tempt fate by absorbing another attack. Her mana pool was already close to full and so such an attack would have nowhere to go if she tried absorbing it. To that, she summoned a mighty glacier that successfully blocked the attack but shattered in doing so.

With a flick of her wrist the pieces of ice that scattered from the blast all came at him from all angles all at once. It was too much for him to avoid. One of the shards shredded his lackluster corporis and ripped through the flesh and muscle of his calf.

He dropped to his knees. Without a stable corporis to protect him Eliza was able to use telekinesis to hold him down enough to where he was only able to protect a small area of his body with flames as another volley of bullets hit him.

"It's over Finch." Eliza said.

"HA!" He laughed right to her face. "I'm an asset, you spoiled brat. Even now, the worst the order you love so dearly would do is lock me up in one of their prisons. And with what I know, someone will bust me out. I could probably even spin it. It'll be my word against yours. Me, a venerated police liaison with friends all over the area who have worked with me for decades. You, a sixteen-year-old kid who The Celestial Order already doesn't like."

"Well, maybe The Celestial Order should be a little less forgiving for human criminals." Eliza said.

"You have no say, no power over me. You're just a pathetic brat clinging to what little power you have hoping that one day daddy will actually acknowledge you. Well newsflash kid, your Celestial Order abandoned you to this godforsaken city. So you might as well just get with the program, let me go and,"

Eliza didn't let him finish his sentence. She impaled his chest with her rapier. The enchantment activated, pumping the inside of his body with enough hot air to pop a normal man like a balloon. His ears ruptured, his eyes bulged out, his veins throbbed and burst, his skin bubbled and tore. And then he popped. Only a small bit of blood splashed onto Eliza's face. The rest of his blood evaporated from the heat all that pressure caused. As what was left of him fell to the ground, Eliza wiped her face clean with a handkerchief.

"You killed him." Captain Claymore said. Eliza looked at the remnants of the corrupt cop at her feet. She realized exactly what she did and instantly tried justifying her actions.

"For someone who carried out criminal activities while working with the Order...I have no mercy!" Eliza scoffed. "Official protocol would have been to let him go, report him to the inquisition and let them take care of it. I admit I let my anger get the best of me but he was still a threat."

"Was that the first time you,"

"Killed someone? Human? Yes. I've killed a demon before. And they're not much different. Demons are just humans with their penchant for evil turned up."

"If you say so." He sighed. "Either way, one of those attacks took out my radio, the car, and your phone."

"That could be an issue." Eliza held her knuckle to her lip. She looked around and saw a twenty-four-hour pharmacy across the street. "I don't suppose they'd have a phone."

"Good idea."

The pharmacy was closed due to the emergency but between the two of them they had no issue getting in and using the phone. A few minutes later Amelia arrived with a full police escort. There was but one issue left to handle. Dodger and Oliver had gone silent after leaving Shadowbrooke so the next destination for these warriors of justice would be to assist them in taking down The Hellfire Brats.

CHAPTER 29

Raid of The Hellfire Brats

Individually The Hellfire Brats were all competent mages that could go toe-to-toe with any knight. They were each incredibly strong considering they had learned how to fight on their own. Together they were a force to be reckoned with. Michael was a strong sonoma-class mage and champion boxer. Marcus was a psychic-class mage quick enough to avoid any direct attack. Meanwhile Sebastian was a caster-class mage and could cover both of them at range.

"You don't have to do this, Crane." Dodger said. The righteous demoran knew that even if Oliver was just as skilled as he was they'd be at a steep disadvantage. "You can still walk away. You owe them nothing."

"It's not about owing them. It's about putting them in a position where they owe me! And you are in no position to negotiate." Sebastian lit his finger on fire and pointed it at Oliver.

"Take cover." Dodger shoved Oliver out of the way as the fireballs came. He dodged the projectiles and batted one back towards Sebastian. Marcus flew behind them and kicked Dodger's back. Oliver fired a quintet of bullets at Sebastian. The first two bullets missed the mark and the third connected to his chest while the fourth and fifth were blocked by Michael.

Michael lunged towards Oliver. Dodger focused on Sebastian and Marcus because he knew exactly what was coming. He threw a ball at Sebastian in a way he knew would be dodged. It bounced off the train car, the building across the way and then right into the side of Sebastian's head. Meanwhile, Dodger used what little bit of ice magic he knew to encase his fist to punch Marcus. The ice exploded on his flaming body and sent him backwards. At the exact same time, Oliver blasted Michael in the chest and sent him flying into The Hellfire Brat's psychic.

Dodger jumped into the air and threw a green fireball at the pair. Marcus dodged the blast and flew towards him as Sebastian did the same. The agent of Nightwatch kicked off the air to avoid them both. Oliver followed up Dodger's evasive maneuver with a powerful animus blast that connected with both fighters. Sebastian was strong enough to take the brunt of the damage on his own thus allowing Marcus to target the younger boy. Dodger knew from experience that the best way to combat a psychic was to divide their attention and aim for a counter attack so he hurled a ball at the blue-flamed demoran. Sebastian wound up his arm to incinerate the fastball but then Dodger punched the air, unleashing the vacuum air cannon he built up with his prior evasive maneuver.

Both mages tumbled to the ground but Dodger's sensus and telekinesis skills were good enough to keep the fastball curving around. Oliver unleashed another wide blast at Marcus, whose body turned into fire to let the blast pass right through him. He reformed his body directly behind Oliver and directly into the path of the oncoming curveball. As soon as Oliver knew what had happened, he spun around and fired a gunshot into Marcus' kneecap. The bullet stung but the demoran's corporis was able to absorb enough of the impact to keep the shot from crippling him.

Neither Marcus nor Oliver were great at hand to hand so the two wrestled on the ground while Dodger found himself fighting Sebastian and Michael. The gangleader conjured a burning purple club while Michael covered his fists in flames. It took an immense amount of focus to dodge everything they threw at him and he had to rely more and more on his own instincts rather than the benefits of future-sight.

"So, your little cronie picked up some tricks eh Dodger?" Sebastian said. "Too bad you're still the same as ever."

Michael landed a blow to Dodger's head at the same time Marcus spun to his feet and kicked Oliver in the chest. Both agents of Nightwatch were struggling and neither one had made a dent. Dodger even tried focusing on the burn mark Oliver left in Michael's chest, but with Sebastian covering the street in burning ash that was proving an impossible task on his own. He was running out of options and Oliver was running out of time.

"Nothing personal kid." Marcus said as he kicked Oliver in the chest, sending him several feet away. "But that Shadow Man isn't here to save you this time."

"Keep him down Marcus." Sebastian said with glee. "Michael and I have the traitor under control."

Michael charged in first. Dodger flipped into the air and smacked him in the head with a bat. The thug jerked back and hit his foe with an elbow. The agent rolled to his feet in time to avoid Sebastian's following magma attack. Dodger had one last trick up his sleeve to try evening the odds. He fired his own green animus blast from his left hand and threw a pair of baseballs with the other. They both avoided the pure energy beam but were beaned in the face by the balls. The next stage in Dodger's plan was to detonate the balls. He had changed the core inside those two balls into plastic explosives. The resulting blast sent both men flying in opposite directions. Finally, Dodger pulled out his pistol and took aim at Sebastian. Of the two he had the weaker corporis and would most likely be undone by one more shot. The agent of Nightwatch took too long and had to hesitate against the trigger.

"Dodger!" Marcus shouted. "Give it up, or I'll do something you'll regret." The demoran had his hand around Oliver's neck. Dodger swore under his breath. If Oliver had only kept up for a few seconds longer Dodger could have evened the odds and destroyed the gang's morale before help arrived.

"Alright asshole." Dodger said as he discarded his gun and raised his hands. There wasn't much else he could do, least not under these circumstances. In this moment Dodger proved himself the better psychic. Psychic mage's couldn't actually see into the future, at least not until they reached levels far higher than any street-tough. What they could do with a level-two sensus and above was sense the thoughts and plans of the people around them. Dodger had been periodically using the basic function of his sensus to scan the area while Marcus used its more advanced functions to keep a thumb pressed on any thought Dodger and Oliver may have. Marcus had no such natural gift of foresight. When he saw Dodger had no more tricks of his own he let his guard down.

Marcus sensed the approaching vehicle too late to make a move. When he did, Oliver latched onto him and held him down. A wave of orange and green flame enveloped them both and was perfectly aimed to hit Marcus without hitting Oliver. Marcus took a lot of damage from that blast and as soon as he broke free of Oliver's grip, he was hit by the boy's animus and sent flying.

Six police cars surrounded the area. Each of them armed to the teeth. Eliza stepped from one of the cars while Amelia leapt from the roof and checked on the boy she had saved yet again. Eliza wasted no time flying directly at Sebastian. She was already thoroughly done with this night and was overcome with a bloodlust the likes of which she had never before.

Sebastian's heel slid along the ground as he avoided the lethal strike. Dodger made the ground more elastic, sending him off balance before he summoned the gun back to his hand and opened fire. The gangleader managed to tank the bullet but was thrust backwards and now had his back against the side of the train.

The tide turned extremely quickly. Marcus tried going after Eliza only to be met with a freezing torrent that extinguished any flames he could summon. Meanwhile Michael did no better in round two against Amelia than he did before. Not only that but the police were all too eager to use lethal force against the demoran gang that had caused so many arsons and unleashed monsters into the city.

"Sebastian, run!" Marcus shouted.

The train whistle blew. The mobsters who were running the train were bailing to safer ground. Sebastian unleashed his animus in a circle, flipping some of the cop cars into the air with Oliver and Dodger along with them. Another wave of his arm burned a pair of officers to a crisp. He then jumped on the train as it left its position.

"We'll clean up here." Eliza said as she pulled both of them off the ground. "Now do what you need to." She threw Dodger directly at the train with her own powerful telekinesis. She then paused as she grabbed Oliver by the shoulder. The blonde boy nodded and they both understood. So with a nod of her own Eliza launched Oliver even harder than she had Dodger.

Eliza wasn't willing to let Dodger handle Sebastian alone. She didn't have enough faith in his talents or his drive. Someone like Oliver who was relatively powerless but still willing to fight was more righteous in her eyes. Before she returned to her duty of subduing the other members of The Hellfire Brats she offered a short prayer that they succeed in returning home in one piece.

CHAPTER 30

Oliver Off Rails

Sebastian quickly made his way to the front of the train. He was livid at himself and his brothers that they were not able to kill Dodger before the knights arrived. Even more than that he was cursing Copper for failing his only job for the night. He had underestimated the arch knight and that same arch knight had vanquished him.

"Do not stop this train for any reason." He told the conductor. "I'm not finished yet." He still had a chance to do things himself. He knew both the stowaways were in just as bad of shape as he was. He just needed to even the odds a little bit. So he cracked open a container housing bottles of little red pills. He had heard this was one of the new things coming out of Baltimore that Allistor Briggs was hoping to distribute around St. Louis.

All it took was one pill and Sebastian was better than ever. He felt the full might of his demoran heritage course through his veins. He felt energized and invincible and only pondered for a second what must have been in them.

Meanwhile Oliver and Dodger had narrowly caught the train and taken out the two guards in the rearmost car. Oliver had hesitated to use his gun. He knew that all these hired goons were bad people but they were still people. He didn't have it in him to kill any of them.

They made their way to the next car and Dodger decided to do some investigating. He cracked open one of the crates and there was a clump of dead leaves and strands of webs. There was also a splattering of fresh blood and some dark fecal circles. Dodger wiped some of the blood with his finger and licked it.

"Hm...blood, not human or demoran ...but sulfuric, definitely something from Sarph." He spat on the floor after making his examination.

"Gross." Oliver gagged.

"Eh don't be a baby." Dodger teased. "This must be how they transported the vampyr's into the city."

"Come to think of it, the monsters we fought looked way different than the one from before."

"Like I said, they're parasitic creatures. The spider part is the only real part. The rest is just what it has incorporated by latching onto various hosts. Or, if it's still fresh and feeding, you can actually remove the parasite and whatever it latched onto can recover."

"Do you think Sebastian knows we're here?" Oliver asked.

"Yeah. And I'm sure he's ready for us." Dodger said.

He led the way into the next car and Sebastian was standing in the middle of the aisle. An estranged smile crossed his lips and his fingers twitched in anticipation. Before either could react, a metal bar sprung up, wrapped around Oliver's wrist and magnetized him to the wall of the car.

"Last chance Sebastian." Dodger said. "Give up now and I'll only kick your ass a little bit."

"Oh, wiping that smug as shit smile off your face will make this all worth it." Sebastian said.

The gangster unleashed a barrage of fireballs from his fingers. Dodger punched the air and countered the barrage with a torrent of green flames. The Nightwatch agent was then blasted back by the colliding flames and Sebastian rushed at him. A bar was flicked into the air and coiled into a ball. Dodger blasted it with his bat and struck the thug. Sebastian melted the iron ball and sent a wave of flames engulfing the entire train car sending

Dodger to his knees. Sebastian had overwhelmed his opponent, grabbed him by the throat and slammed him down.

"Damn it." Oliver huffed as he tried breaking free.

"Can't live up to your name and dodge my attacks in a place like this." Sebastian said. "Just like you to try avoiding any consequences."

"I'm not the one who started a bunch of fires and is trying to get away with it."

"I'm a survivor, Dodger!" Sebastian punched him in the face. "And as soon as I'm done with you, I'm going to get Marcus and Michael back and we'll run this town."

He and Dodger got into a contest of raw power. Flames licked all around them. Meanwhile Oliver's body began to convulse as he tried prying the bar from around his wrists. His muscles popped as he ripped one of his arms free of the bonds. His vision filled with light as he unleashed an animus blast into Sebastian's chest. The demon landed with a bone cracking thud against the car door and Oliver was free.

"I'm sick of you two. Just die already!" Sebastian howled as he summoned more violet flames.

Sebastian blasted a hole in the bottom of the car. The flames melted the track and the whole train began to shake. There was a thud and a screech. The whole car started to tilt and Oliver hit his head against the window cracking the glass. All three stomachs churned as the car did a full flip and dislodged itself from the rest of the train.

In a flash the car exploded off the rails. Smoke and flames filled the agents' lungs. The fires etched hotter and hotter. By the time Oliver tumbled out of the car he was coughing and delirious.

Next came a violet haze. Everything burned. The flames completely engulfed the young boy's body. He had no corporis to absorb the damage. Dodger was too hurt to pull him out. He was in more pain than ever before.

His flesh started to melt. His scream broke and turned into a gargle. Next came a fiery light. Then nothing.

But darkness.

Rage.

And an overwhelming power that defies an adequate explanation.

CHAPTER 31

High Level Combat

The majority of mages only stuck to the basics: telekinesis, pyrokinesis, aquakinesis and using the tria-ethos. More advanced mages would pick two or so techniques and apply them in a variety of ways. Eliza specialized in controlling temperature and pressure. Dodger specialized in making things elastic. Sir Nightwatch was a cut above all of them. He had his specialties that he relied on in all his fights but he was also able to learn from his opponents and add their skills to his own.

In his storied career battling evil he had fought Bartleby of the Storm no less than five times before vanquishing him. In those clashes he had taken Bartleby's epithet for himself and learned how to conjure massive violent storms.

He did so as he approached his new quarry. Ever since he entered St. Louis, he had been tracking the host's movements. Sir Nightwatch had a reliable network of informants at his beck and call. One of them was a cameraman for Blackfire News and had relayed the host's schedule to Sir Nightwatch all this time.

It was this same informant who had once seen Damien Crow turn a blackmailer to ash using black flames. Another informant within the celestial inquisition stated that The Celestial Order was aware of his abilities but didn't bother with him. The Celestial Order lived by the grace of public opinion and so they ignored any rumors about his underhanded dealings.

Sir Nightwatch had done his research. Damien Crow was born wealthy so it wouldn't be unspeakable if his family kept him out of The Celestial Order's reach. If he took an interest in magic then there wouldn't be much that could stop him from pursuing such craft.

More importantly he was the lynchpin in this operation the agents of Nightwatch had stumbled upon. While Sir Nightwatch had full faith in his agents' abilities, they had too much on their plate to take it all on alone. So he took it upon himself to take Damien Crow off the air permanently.

Damien Crow had bought out an entire hotel, no doubt with the mob's money, and had filled it with his own army of thugs as well as a whole pack of ghouls. Ghouls themselves were another monster that were more of a pest on their own. They were hairless gray primates that primarily ate fish. These ones in particular were spliced together with vampyrs to strengthen their bodies and make them more aggressive towards humans.

Sir Nightwatch perched atop a tower as the storm rolled in. His stratagem had been completed. There was too great a chance the hired help had no idea what was going on or the true nature of the man they were hired to protect. Damien Crow was the only one the shadow of justice would swallow up.

There were three floors with guards. The lobby was full of monsters, shambling around. Sir Nightwatch's celestial compass couldn't detect them but his sensus could. Upon inspection, he surmised that this was because of scent disruptors that were placed on the middle floor. As the name suggests, scent disruptors produce a clean smelling odor created from particles that bind to the particles that produce the scent of everything that comes from Sarph.

Halfway up the building were half a dozen guards with guns and night vision binoculars. They were the lookouts and protectors of the scent disruptors. They would be Sir Nightwatch's first targets. Taking the scent disruptors silently would alert Eliza Alcius and the police to the monsters' presence without alerting Damien Crow to the mage's.

Last but not least was the penthouse. Damien Crow himself was there, looking at a laptop. That machine was the key to taking down Damien Crow and all his co-conspirators. It had all the paperwork on it, uploading and preparing to turn the series of extortions and scams into business fronts for all his criminal operations in the city. With his objectives in mind, Sir Nightwatch made his move. He flew under the cover of darkness and suspended himself over the balcony where one of the guards was about to be standing.

Shadows extended from the master mage's cloak and snatched up the poor unsuspecting guard and covered his mouth to keep him from screaming. Before he knew what was happening, he was knocked out and suspended against the wall of the building.

The second guard was passing by the balcony. He saw that his friend wasn't where he was supposed to be and walked onto the balcony where the full weight of this raptoral mage dropped down on him.

The next three were patrolling together. The shadowy owl sprinted down the hallway and around the corner. He threw a fist into the first one's head, sending him through the wall. The next took an elbow to the shoulder and a punch to the temple. The third was the only one who had time to react. He spun and pointed the machine gun at the attacker but before he knew to pull the trigger his gun was kicked into the air falling into the waiting glove of Sir Nightwatch. One whip of the shadows later and all three were completely unconscious.

The final guard protecting the scent disruptor heard the noise and left his post to investigate. He turned the corner and saw his three comrades beaten and strewn along the floor. Panicked hands reached for his radio but they never made it. He was ripped off the floor and sent into the ceiling by an invisible enemy that filled him with brief terror before he was welcomed by the sweet embrace of sleep.

Sir Nightwatch had reached the scent disruptor. The pinkish crystal sat along a copper rod with two screws connecting the shaft to the gem.

The mage reached into his cloak and removed a small package from his person. He gently placed the black box at the base of the disruptor and let it be for the time being.

Silky shadows pried the elevator door open. The owl-like mage gazed into the dark abyss that laid before him. Anyone else would have seen nothing but darkness and death. The boss of Nightwatch saw the next stage of his plan. He dropped down the shaft and readied his Reflected Sphere Generator. Damien Crow in all his life had yet to learn this valuable lesson. Any defensive measure had its weakness. So long as the scent disruptor was operational he would not be able to monitor the ghouls using a celestial compass. And thanks to the vast distance between the floors Sir Nightwatch could ensnare all those at the bottom within the Reflected Sphere while Crow was none the wiser.

Landing on the elevator at the bottom disturbed the ghouls shambling around the lobby. Sir Nightwatch then fired up the Reflected Sphere and got to work. He came out of the elevator guns blazing. He controlled the trajectory of each bullet to hit the ghouls in the head and did so with enough speed and precision that he emptied the clips from both his guns before the creatures could react.

He returned the guns to their holsters and drew his sword. With two swings, the closest monster was bisected and beheaded. With no more ghouls in immediate range he took a second to toss fresh clips into the air and slam them into his pistols. As he let another volley of bullets fly he charged off the edge into the balcony. He kept moving, whipping his shadows around and sending bullets to make quick work of the ghouls. He ran up a pillar back onto the upper level and removed a ghoul's head from its shoulders then kicked it into a crowd of monsters as he commanded the flying bullets to finish off the final batch. Only one remained and Sir Nightwatch wrapped it in threads of shadows for one last bit of theatrics to make his grand entrance.

Damien Crow had been in his penthouse the entire time. His finger tapped at the laptop waiting for any word from his employees. If things had gone well, Eliza Alcius would be dead, Sebastian would be wrapping up and the train with all the supplies for their criminal empire would be making its way to Shadowbrooke. There was one thing the journalist couldn't shake off. He was wondering if this Sir Nightwatch really existed.

Then lightning struck the building. Power to the entire structure went out. The little black box that had been placed fried the scent disruptor. For just a second two dozen signals appeared on his compass, then two, then one. Then the door was kicked open. Another bolt of lightning flashed through the window but did not illuminate anything beyond the door. Nothing except two burning orange eyes.

"So…you are real." Damien Crow whispered as he stood up. "Nightwatch I presume?" Even with his finely tuned sensus he could barely perceive anything through the thick shadows aside from the coursing orange power of the man who hid within them.

"I am but one man." Sir Nightwatch's voice echoed from everywhere and nowhere all at once. "Nightwatch is a movement that will eat away at the hypocrisy of these worlds." Damien Crow had ultimately been caught off guard. His only hope was to either destroy the laptop or destroy this mage that had hounded him. "Whereas a tongue like yours only sows discord."

"Discord? My words are the only ones that matter. I tell the world what the truth is. And once you're disposed of the world will know that you were an assassin sent by The Celestial Order to silence me."

"Truth is absolute. I will expose your lies."

"Over my dead body."

"That's the idea."

"Murder? What makes you any better than me?"

"There is good and there is evil …your heart is as black as your flames. Evil should not be allowed to take root." Understanding the seriousness of this mage's code, Damien Crow was prepared to destroy the laptop. That way, even if he were to fail at besting this mage, he and his co-conspirators would remain in the shadows. "I wouldn't do that if I were you."

He swung his fist down only for the laptop to be pulled out of his reach and hidden within the folds of Sir Nightwatch's cloak. Black flames flung from the journalists fingers but were blocked by threads of shadow. He sprinted around the wall of threads but his foe had already rolled out of the cover and fired a pair of bullets through the defensive binds.

Damien Crow covered his entire body in black flame and shoved Sir Nightwatch against the wall. In a boxing match they were evenly matched. Sir Nightwatch could not get a grip on the criminal as long as the black flames coated his body. Meanwhile Damien Crow lacked the combat experience to land a decisive blow. The upperhand went to Sir Nightwatch, as the bullets he fired earlier shattered the glass and cleared the way for another bolt of lightning guided by its conjurer to strike the black-flamed crime lord.

Sir Nightwatch cackled as he beat the man senseless after that. Damien Crow tried burning everything down only to have his flames swallowed up by the torrent of rain that poured in from the window. Without his flames he could do nothing to stop Sir Nightwatch's threads. One bundle of threads smacked him in the mouth and grabbed his tongue.

Damien Crow knew he was beat. He dropped to his knees and raised his hands. Orange eyes contemplated the man's fate for a moment as the sound of sirens fast approached. For a fleeting moment he thought of sparring the fool. Then again, he had connections, influence, he was savvy enough to play dumb and charismatic enough to escape justice. So Sir Nightwatch did what he was always bound to do in this situation. He stopped the rain, turned the water drenching the man into combustible fuel, ripped the man's tongue out and ignited him.

Damien Crow's last words were a muffled scream of burning agony as everything he had done to this city was done unto him. For his crimes

Sir Nightwatch took pity on him and kicked him out the window. The journalist had once been the hottest commentator on TV. Now he was nothing but a pile of smoldering ash on the streets of St. Louis.

Perched on the building like an owl he did not laugh at this victory yet. Deep into the city in the direction of the railway was a radiant yellow glow. A deep sense of foreboding and urgency took hold of the shadowy mage. While he had been battling Damien Crow his newest agent was in great peril.

CHAPTER 32

The Death and Rebirth of Oliver Turner

It wasn't everyday that a homerun clinched the game in the bottom of the ninth. The violet firestorm should have been the last strike. Oliver Turner had been consumed by a blast capable of melting human flesh. Yet he stood with hair singed and skin charred. The boy was alive yet dead at the same time. His eyes were whitted out, blood pussed and dried and cracked along the worst of his burns.

"How the hell are you still alive?" Sebastian hissed.

"Oliver?" Dodger raised his voice, for he knew Sebastian had raised an excellent question.

No response came from Oliver, least not immediately. The last vestiges of his chains had been burned away. He was now unbound just as his parents had feared. What stood there in front of the smoldering remains of the train car was the precise reason why he had been kept away from magic–kept away from his own powers–for so long and why it was imperative that he began his training when he did and not a moment sooner nor later.

His skin started to rip and regenerate as his body doubled in size. The blood that now flowed freely from his veins shredded his skin and molded him into a beast befitting of his true inheritance. Yes, all mages had heard the stories. Oliver Turner's kind were an abomination to both human and demoran, a race with no place to call home. They were creatures born from the unlawful union of the two races yet loved by neither. Cursed beings whose average life expectancy was only five years. The ones who did manage to survive the worst of their frequent adolescent illnesses and learned to harness their power were destined to change the fate of the world. Oliver Turner was a nephilim.

"What the hell are you?" Sebastian shouted. His purple flames returned to his side and then he sent another blast at Oliver. Dodger tried to intercept the flames, to do what he failed to do before and protect his partner but it was unnecessary as it was futile. Oliver's shriek extinguished the flames and sent Dodger flying in the opposite direction.

A golden yellow light shined through with such potency that it replaced Oliver's skin. His back tore open–spraying more blood as it did– and sprouted a pair of feathery wings. Not only was Oliver's mother a demoran, she too descended from one of the avian tribes. The one that had been weak amateurish Oliver Turner was now the pinnacle of biology. But therein lies a terrible cost. A mage's corporis is what gave their body strength, protected them from their own spells, and allowed them to sustain such transformations. Oliver Turner's own power was killing him.

"Oliver buddy, calm down!" Dodger's words failed him. The rage of the nephilim had been unleashed.

Rocks and dust were kicked up from his first launching step. Sebastian could see it coming with his sensus, but he couldn't react in time. Oliver was fast, faster than a bullet. And that amount of momentum slapped Sebastian into a stationary train car with enough force to flip it over.

Sebastian sent a torrent of flame towards Oliver. The kid raised a golden claw that blocked the approaching inferno. He sprinted over to The Hellfire Brat with enough speed to outpace his sensus, grabbed him by the head and slammed him into the gravel then threw him overhead towards the overpass.

Sebastian sprouted flaming wings to stay in the air. A dozen balls of flame manifested around him. These fireballs combined with dust and gravel to form mini-meteors. He strained and grunted, pushing his hands towards Oliver urging each meteor to strike with the speed of a cannonball.

The projectiles pummeled Oliver into the ground. The nephilim rose to his feet only to be engulfed in a flaming twister. He then blew the twister away with a single blast from his hand. Sebastian crossed his arms and turned the charred gravel into spikes that pierced Oliver's sides, back and stomach. Even that wasn't enough to subdue the nephilim. He broke free of the spikes with another roar. Under any other circumstance a mage would be impressed with Sebastian's control. He fought with skill and power that could rival most members of The Celestial Order. Alas this battle was testament to the reason even the most legendary mages often died in battle against mindless behemoths or leviathans.

In his rage Oliver Turner had turned into a monster. He acted only on instinct. There was no logic, no intelligence behind his eyes. He was a monster the caliber of which neither Dodger nor Sebastian had ever seen. It was when this nephilim emerged unscathed from Sebastian's meteor attack that The Hellfire Brats' boss realized he was in serious trouble.

The wings of the nephilim kicked up more dust as he flew into Sebastian's gut like a spear causing the demoran to vomit from the impact. Oliver grabbed him by his shaggy hair. In desperation, Sebastian kicked the nephilim in the neck. Oliver retaliated by blasting him into the ground.

Sebastian hit the ground so hard, chunks of gravel embedded into his back. The ground split and a small crater formed from the impact. Sebastian clenched his fist towards the sky. In an instant, the oxygen around Oliver cooked away. The fumes were noticeably noxious. Olver, or what was left of Oliver, started clawing at his own face and throat until drops of shimmering blood rained down from the young man.

All Dodger could do was watch in horror and try replenishing the oxygen Sebastian was erasing. Had Oliver been even remotely conscious such an attack would have no effect. He'd merely hold his breath and move faster than Sebastian's spell could keep up. This beast that had sprung fully formed from Oliver was desperate to catch its breath before it made any such move.

"Oliver, listen to me!" Dodger's only hope was to appeal to some kind of intelligence in the nephilim. Whether it was Oliver's human logic or something more primal and instinctual didn't matter. The only way to help him was to get him to help himself.

Oliver screamed to the sky. Golden light radiated from all his pores. The entire city could see the light as Oliver conjured and hurled spears from the sky. Such an ability denoted a level-two animus and yet Oliver was such a natural born caster that he was doing it in his current form. He created his own barrier which relinquished Sebastian's atmospheric control and allowed the nephilim to breathe once again.

Violet flames surrounded him and formed the shape of a bird but none could penetrate Oliver's shell. It was trembling with a power that severed the mage's connection to any spells within its sphere. He was now playing defense, no longer actively chasing Sebastian. Instead, he hid in the sphere of his own making and began withering away to the jaws of death.

Sebastian ran off the second he realized he was no longer in active danger. Dodger had to make the choice between stopping the gang leader or saving his friend. He didn't have much time to choose. Sebastian was gaining distance and Oliver's mana was plummeting. Just then, the storm that had been brewing overhead crackled with life. A silver flash was followed by a pillar of orange light that tore through Oliver's shell and forced the nephilim to the ground. As the light faded it was replaced by a shadowy form of Sir Nightwatch. Each finger of his gloved hand worked to absorb all the excess manag radiating from the creature while a vile of blue liquid was injected into his throat.

"Go after Crane." Sir Nightwatch ordered. He controlled each cell in the boy's body to return to the shape they had once held. Dodger put his faith in his boss and did his duty to chase after Sebastian Crane.

He located Oliver's discarded gun and began chasing Sebastian down. Both mages were tired. Both had taken some heavy hits. Both knew that when it came down to it, this battle would end with whoever shot first. Dodger had to harden his resolve. If Sebastian Crane escaped he'd never step foot in St. Louis again. He did his job well enough to get all illegal merchandise out of the city before the police arrived. Even with how many of the co-conspirators were doomed to be tried and convicted, the mob could rebuild so long as they had Sebastian and everything on that train.

Dodger followed him all the way to Poplar St. Bridge. Dodger did not wait to get any closer. He fired a bullet into the thug's leg, making him fall to the side. By the time he got back up, Dodger was right next to him, pointing the gun at him.

"So this is how it ends, eh Dodger?" He wheezed.

"I'm taking you in."

"Why? So that I can be executed by The Celestial Order just for being a demon? To hell with that. Shoot me ...coward."

"Trying to save your life isn't cowardice, you piece of shit."

"We were so close to creating a world where we wouldn't have to worry about The Celestial Order." Sebastian said. "The Celestial Order can be bought, persuaded, but that requires a lot of money and the backing of someone like Damien Crow."

"You daft bastard, you were being used by Crow." Dodger said. "Not that it matters. Sir Nightwatch showing up when he did means that Damien Crow is dead."

"Do you really think you're so much better for being used by that Nightwatch dude? And working with The Celestial Order? The same order that killed your parents?"

"That's where we could never see eye to eye Sebasian. I never really knew my parents. I never cared about what kind of blood runs through your veins. Doesn't make you any more or less an asshole."

"The noble individualist." He laughed again. "I'd rather it end this way than spend a few weeks in prison before being beheaded."

The last vestiges of Dodger's sensus saw the flames coming. As soon as Sebastian wound his body to pitch the fire ball, he was hit by a bullet. The chunk of metal cracked against his sternum and sent him over the edge of the bridge. He tumbled into the waters of the mighty Mississippi and vanished from Dodger's view within seconds.

The victor leaned against the railings. The pain from the constant battle and following trainwreck finally took their toll. He passed out there, waiting for someone to take him home. As he dreamt he pondered Oliver's fate and whether the knights were enough to handle the rest. Meanwhile in the waking world the sound of a motorcycle crept closer.

The rider's gloved hands checked for his vital signs before breathing a sigh of relief. She removed her helmet and let her long locks fall behind her back. She looked around for any signs of life before holstering her rifle and strapping the young man to her motorcycle. Before getting on her bike she rested her head on Dodger's and whispered important words.

"I got your back Dodger. I always will." Even in his sleep the words of Brittany Rembrandt reached his ears.

CHAPTER 33

The Final Report

When Eliza walked into her office she was greeted by a silhouette of a man she hadn't seen in a long time. The tall thin man had silvery white hair, finely styled. His suit was pristine and pure as snow. A thick white mustache covered his lip. On his collar were four shield pendants denoting his rank as paladin. His trusted blade hung loosely off his hip. He didn't turn to meet her gaze at first. Instead he looked out the window and glanced at the file she had on Dodger.

"Father?" She asked.

"It is I, Arch Night Eliza Alcius." His tone and the way he addressed her clued her into the fact that this was not a cordial visit. He was here on business. As such whatever familial feelings they may share didn't matter to him. Her being his daughter was secondary to the fact he was two ranks above her.

"Sorry, Paladin Henry Alcius." Eliza bowed.

"Good to see that your time in flyover country hasn't completely destroyed your manners." Sir Henry Alcius mused. "Now, while you should refrain from acting overly familiar with me while on official business you don't have to be entirely formal."

"Yes of course father." She bowed again.

"I'd prefer Sir." He said. Eliza understood why he would cling to that more than his official title. He had been given his promotions within the knights' branch of The Celestial Order with very little fuss. The titles of Sir and Dame were not so easy to come by. Only a mage who had been instrumental in dealing with a great threat were given those titles.

"Of course Sir." It also made her think of Sir Nightwatch. Surely that wasn't his name. He must have done something very specific to acquire that title and that was just one mystery Eliza would like to solve someday.

"Eliza, you showed cleverness, resourcefulness and strength in dealing with this threat." The paladin took a seat at Eliza's desk and rested his elbows upon its top. His azure gaze looked out from the tops of his fingers as he looked through her more than he looked at her. "Yet as per the code of The Celestial Order I cannot condone your use of civilian help in solving this matter."

That was enough to break what joy Eliza had felt at her father's presence. She didn't give him a chance to respond. Instead she took her final report and slammed it down in front of him. Her outburst gave the seasoned mage a moment of pause to glance at the contents of the file.

"Maybe I wouldn't have to if the rest of The Celestial Order did their damn jobs!" Sir Henry Alcius had seen this scowl more times than he could count. Nearly every time he had taken her to meet a member of the Grand Council it ended with this exact same glare. Yet this was the first time a scowl so intense had been directed at him. "All of this was the result of Chicago crime syndicates. Tell Deacon Mills that if I have to clean up after her mess one more time I will see to it that her retirement from the knights is accompanied with her funeral."

"Are you threatening your superior officer?"

"I'm telling that incompetent tart to do her damn job."

"She has served this order for many years. We are too few to chase down every mobster. There are those within our ranks that believe you made things worse."

"What is that supposed to mean?"

"Your insistence on bringing these men in yourself is what led to them taking such drastic measures." Sir Henry Alcius made no indication of his feelings on the matter. "Plus, the inquisition is going to hold a formal hearing over your actions against Clint Finch."

"That bastard was a traitor!"

"Know your place Arch Knight Alcius! That man was still an associate of The Celestial Order. You had no right to dish out justice without a formal inquiry. Eliza, I thought you more than anyone respected the code."

"To hell with the code if it keeps me from doing my job."

"I have no opinion on the matter. My standing only allows me to relay the thoughts of our peers. If not for me it would be them taking you in, by force if necessary. You are to meet at the St. Louis courthouse to state your case. Until then, say nothing more of the matter. The inquisition will decide what punishment you get if any."

"Is that all, father?"

"I'm sorry but in matters of the celestial inquisitors my hands are completely tied." The older knight shrugged. "There is one other thing I wished to say to you, not as a paladin, but as your father." The tall man rose from his seat and grabbed the file he had been looking at before. "I don't want you being involved with this Nightwatch. If he has agents working in this city I have no choice but to allow you to work with them as you see fit. Such is the perk of your rank. But when it comes to Sir Nightwatch himself, leave him be. Do not work with him and never work against him. Both will only lead to your destruction. If you are asked, play ignorant. Pretend you never heard of the man."

"I will not bother asking why then." Eliza understood that much. There was some hope knowing that the most sensible thing her father said was the one thing he said as her father.

After that, Sir Henry Alcius took his leave. He had other matters to attend to regarding the various arch knights and deacons within their ranks. Eliza meanwhile breathed a sigh of relief. Sebastian Crane's body had never been found, the other members of his gang along with other members of the fledgling crime syndicate had been apprehended. There were just two other matters to attend to.

The first was finding a new police liaison. Typically the inquisition handled all logistical matters of this kind but Eliza would make it very clear she wished for Captain Johnathan Claymore. He had proven his valor, saved her life and if not for his quick thinking they would have lost Donovan Brown's file to Clint Finch's attack on the politician. If the inquisition would indulge her request and if the captain would accept her offer he would make for a great asset. Not to mention he trusts her and knows why she felt the need to kill her previous liaison.

Then there was the matter of Sir Nightwatch. As if the embodiment of fate heard her quandary and sought to answer it, she felt a presence looming in the street. She went outside to investigate and at first saw nothing. It was the middle of the night so the street lights should have been on. Yet there wasn't a sign of light to be seen. Not even from the moon and stars.

"Your sensus is finely tuned." The voice seemed to come from all around. After a second Eliza was able to trace it to its source to the top one of the light posts where two burning amber spheres hovered in the darkness. She drew the Moon Piercer from its sheath and pointed it at the spheres. A single light kicked on and she was finally able to see the mass of shadows bound with a silver scarf that seemed to loom over her entire being.

"Sir Nightwatch I presume?" Eliza said.

"You presume…correctly." Sir Nightwatch didn't appear human but Eliza couldn't detect anything otherworldly about him other than his appearance. No matter how hard she looked she could not spot any distinguishing features about his face. It was as if his whole visage shifted depending on where her focus was. "I'm sure you have questions, but know that I am not obliged to answer any of them."

"I just have two that I need to know for now." Eliza said. "Are you the one that notified the police and asked for my involvement?"

"Yes...and no. I am the one who willed it to be but I did not call them myself. It was another one of my agents, acting on my orders. When I discovered Damien Crow was involved I feared my agents, even with your help, would not be enough to deal out justice."

"And if you're here I'll assume you're the one who killed Damien Crow as well. That brings me to my other question. Are you on our side?" He took a lot longer to answer that one. As he stood, more of his features came into focus: a large hawkish nose, pale skin, and crows feet on his eyes.

"Yes...and no. I have grown tired of The Celestial Order and their... stench of hypocrisy. A stench that has yet to infect you Eliza Alcius. Your continued cooperation with my agents is testament to that. We are not allies, but we both work for the betterment of civilization."

"Is that all?"

"No. I came here to ask that you continue aiding Oliver Turner in his growth. He possesses a great power. One that, now that word will spread, will make him a target. I came here to warn you that beings far greater than Damien Crow will come. I will not be able to be here all the time to look out for him."

"I'll keep an eye out." Eliza nodded. "But not because you asked me to. Oliver Turner is a citizen of this county, and therefore under my protection as arch knight."

"I see ...you are still clearly young and have a long way to go. I hope you do not turn down the wrong path, and substitute your ideology with your legalistic duty."

The lights flickered again and he was gone. A second later the stars and moon returned and the lights turned back on. Eliza was left staring at the lone street light, mulling over what she had heard until Amelia returned from her errand.

"I take it things went well." Amelia said as she checked on her partner. She had gotten quite skilled at reading Eliza's emotions and the fact the arch knight was not fuming meant that the conversation with her father wasn't horrible.

"Despite what father says, I will not merely allow Dodger and Oliver to work for some mystery mage unchecked. This does not leave this room but I sense a greater deal of importance with my being here than I ever had before. We will find out more about Sir Nightwatch and we will do so without the inquisition knowing."

"Of course Eliza." Amelia said with a bow. "I will do all that you ask."

"This little alliance could work to my advantage. I could take down threats no ordinary arch knight could. If the coming storm is that bad, I will brave it and become a legend. My dream is firmly in my sight. And I still have over a year left before I take my next step."

CHAPTER 34

Blood of the Nephilim

O f all those who were wounded in what would later be known as
The Hellfire Riot, none had received injuries like Oliver Turner.
Yet despite the massive burn marks, broken bones and lacerated
muscles he had made a full recovery. The doctors who had watched over
him called it a miracle. Even the most advanced of medicinal magics can
only speed up natural healing processes and sew tissue back together in a
way that leaves scars.

Oliver had been in a coma whenever he arrived at the hospital and
he remained as such for a week. In that time he dreamed of another life. He
had been so happy in that other life that when he returned to the waking
world he was consumed by a sense of dread. The memories of those dreams
faded as he recalled everything that had happened.

"You're awake." The piercing voice of Sir Nightwatch beckoned from
his bedside. Even when paying a cordial visit he remained in the garb in
which he fought.

"Do you always look like you're cosplaying a pulp hero?" Oliver
groaned. He gave no response to the tease. Instead he closely examined
Oliver's body for himself, as if consuming that which he knew but shut-
tered to believe. "How long was I out?" Oliver asked.

"One Week." Sir Nightwatch said.

"And you've been here the whole time?"

"Most of it. You've made a number of acquaintances in your time here. Any one of them could tell you what all happened but there are things that only I know to tell you."

"Thanks, for taking time out of your schedule for a screw up like me." Oliver lamented.

"We all fall, Oliver Turner. Had you started at the same age I did, you'd be a force to be reckoned with."

"Then why didn't I start early? If you knew my mom then you knew of me. Why did you wait?"

"It wasn't safe." He whispered. "It never is for your type. Your inheritance, if tapped into at too early of an age can lead to...unpleasant consequences. And your mother had far too many enemies to let your presence be known before it was safe."

"But you said it's never safe."

"On your own? No. I had no one willing and able to watch over you until now."

"Dodger." Oliver realized. Their mutual master nodded in agreement. This was just as much a test for the older boy as it had been for the younger nephilim.

"He was my first recruit. Everything moved according to my design. You, Dodger, Eliza, this city, this time, all according to a grand design. It was the best way to handle someone of your inheritance."

"Inheritance this. Inheritance that. What do you mean? What was my mother? What am I?"

What Sir Nightwatch said next was said with a dramatic weight that nearly crushed the entirety of Oliver's being. He did much more than merely answer the question. He gave Oliver a glimpse at just how incomprehensibly large the world could be at times.

"You are the son of William Turner and Daphnella Aurora…a powerful mage of the Angellum clan within the avian tribe …and one of the legendary Seven Threads of Fate born in Sarph."

"You mean she was …?"

"A demoran, like Dodger, but far more powerful than any monster you've met yet. Making you, a nephilim, a hybrid creature."

As Oliver caught up with everything that happened after his transformation it felt increasingly distant from what he previously believed about himself. It still did not feel real to him. He was also learning how far he had left to go. A mage's corporis is what allowed them to undergo transformations. If Oliver transformed just two more times without a corporis he would be finished. That amount of power would be the death of him.

"How long will that take?" Oliver asked.

"Patience Oliver Turner. There is no greater test than patience. There is no greater trial than time. No greater judge than hindsight. And no greater journey than the ever present ticking of a clock."

"Waiting to figure out my own powers might be worse than facing down Marcus again."

"A wise summation." Sir Nightwatch said as he stood. "After you are released from the hospital, Dodger will continue your training." He slid the window open and put his foot on the sill. "Keep your relationship with Eliza and Amelia close to the chest. Help them, let them help you, but don't trust them."

"Why?" Oliver asked. "They're good people. Why would I use them and not trust them?"

"They might bear no ill will towards you…but others in The Celestial Order will. There may come a day when their hands are simply tied and they are unable to help you." He put his other foot on the sill and leaned out. "Others will come, stronger than before. Word of your power has reached the ears of the underworld and the otherworld. Be weary of all of those who come to you as brethren. That is all." With that final warning he fell out of the window and took to the night sky.

Then, just as abruptly as he had first appeared in Oliver's life, Sir Nightwatch was gone. Oliver was forced to pretend that he was a normal teenager yet again despite knowing he was anything but. He would get chewed out by his father, pulled into social excursions by Rachel, trained by Dodger and watched over by Eliza. Everything else was up to him. Feigning a normal life while leading an exceptional one was a task he was eager to get back to. Thus was his choice as an agent of Nightwatch. Which is exactly what he wanted and precisely what he needed. For as the legends state, there will come a day where he too may hold the fate of the world in his grasp.